HUNTER'S REDEMPTION

ELENI P. SIANIS

Fulton Books, Inc.
Meadville, PA

Published by Fulton Books 2020

"Some of the characters, places, and events in
this story are real but have been fictionalized
(imaginary details added or some facts changed)."

ISBN 978-1-64654-305-2 (paperback)
ISBN 978-1-64654-306-9 (digital)

CHAPTER 1

MASON

They are from another world, another way of life that somehow has merged with our own. These worlds are kept separate for the safety of everyone. And yet, I connect them.
—Meredith T. Taylor, *Churning Waters*

As Mason Hunter looks down at his worn black Converse sneakers, each step crackles and crunches down a colorful leaf-strewn sidewalk of Peaks Island, a neighborhood within the city of Portland. If only he had someone to walk with. If he could choose anyone, who would it be? Mason imagines himself with a group of boys from his hockey team who always hang out together. He has tried a few times to get into their clique but always awkwardly messes up. Like the time he worked up the nerve to join in as they jumped up and into each other in a playful way, but when Mason did it, his head hit one of the guys under the chin, causing him to bite his tongue. The fun game was over, and each of them gave Mason an annoyed glance. If they were here now, maybe Mason could talk to them the way they talk so casually to each other. Would they talk about hockey or girls? Mason smiles as he imagines he would say something funny and they would all laugh and pat him on the back. Suddenly, Mason trips a little on an uneven part of the sidewalk, and his mind snaps back to the present. He continues walking and feels embarrassed as if people could hear his thoughts.

His loneliness vanquishes for a while as he arrives at the port to watch ferries carrying passengers from Portland to Forest City Landing at Peaks Island. This day does not seem different from any other. However, one tourist in particular catches Mason's attention. In his midtwenties and walking hand in hand with a beautiful young woman, the man exudes an intense confidence and power. Mason notices the man's expensive watch. A Rolex? How incredible it would be if Mason were rich and famous and could buy whatever frivolous thing he wanted. Then he notices a few people whispering about the man before one of them approaches and asks for an autograph. The man smiles and signs his name very nonchalantly.

Mason leans against a pole and examines the man. His smile looks more like a smirk. Mason can't see his eyes under sunglasses, but it is nonetheless obvious by his casual demeanor that signing autographs is run of the mill for him. Mason imagines that he is in this man's shoes. Fame. How incredible it would be to be famous. Fame means love, acceptance, adoration, and wealth to show the world how truly powerful one is. Is the man an actor? An athlete? It doesn't matter. What does matter is that no one looks down on, rejects, or bullies a famous person. To be famous must be the most incredible feeling in the world.

The man and his girlfriend walk away, and Mason looks around the port. In most of the tourists' faces, he sees a peaceful contentedness that eludes him. They rent bikes or golf carts with Island Tours and go for rides to admire ocean views and homes like Mason's that trace the shore. The visitors rarely stay longer than a few hours. Nonetheless, for a limited period of time, Peaks Island is alive and active with strangers who do not know Mason and the alienating reputation his family of mediums has. By nightfall, the tourists board the ferry, head back with their families, friends, or lovers to the mainland, and Peaks Island resumes its stale mannequin existence.

Heading back home, Mason approaches the home of Trent Stellar, his tormentor for the past three years. Now in their senior year of high school, Mason still walks on the opposite side of the street to avoid any close confrontation. Nonetheless, the thought of Trent always brings back painful memories. Mason remembers his first week of high school when Trent came up to him, pretending to be a friend.

With a smile on his face, Trent said, "Hi, are you Mason Hunter? I've heard a lot about you."

Mason remembers his naive feeling of relief to have someone approach him in a friendly manner. "Yes, I am. How do you know my name? Are we in homeroom together?"

"No, we are not in homeroom together. It's just that I can always spot a freak." Trent bursts into laughter as he nudged Mason in the shoulder and walked away.

Now, only a block away from home, the usual suspects already begin looming around Mason. He doesn't look up but senses the faint shapes moving slowly. In small, quaint towns like Peaks Island, there is always a nosy or bored neighbor watching from a front porch or living room window. Mason wants to yell at these supernatural things to go away, but someone would see, and the gossip would begin anew about how one of the Hunters is talking to ghosts again. Yet he can't stand these strange, ghostly figures following him any longer. They look like regular people, but Mason knows they are deceased and trying to reach him in the hopes that he can help them with some unresolved issue. Usually, the deceased who visit Mason died while in a quarrel with loved ones and beg him to contact those loved ones with an apologetic message.

"Can you help me? I can't rest unless you help me," a twentysomething-year-old man says.

"I don't do that. You have the wrong Hunter. Stop following me."

"But, you *can* help me."

"It doesn't matter! I don't care!" Mason shouts as he stops in his tracks and turns to yell at the ghost, "Go AWAY!"

Just then, Mr. Hamel opens his creaky screen door and stands on his porch looking at Mason with arms folded across his chest. Mason looks at him, and Mr. Hamel just shakes his head in a disapproving manner. Mrs. Hamel steps outside, and Mason can see the husband whispering to his wife about the "crazy Hunter kid."

Great, more gossip, Mason thinks as he picks up his pace. What an idiot he was to speak to a ghost in public like that. When he is out of the Hamels' sight, Mason quickly looks around to make sure no one is watching, and he kicks a garbage can on the side of the road, knocking it over and spilling trash everywhere. It feels good to make a mess for someone else to deal with.

Finally, he is almost home. This time of year, the path that leads to the Hunters' front door is lined with beautiful cabbages and mums in deep oranges and yellows interwoven with over-grown kale plants. Although it is mid-October, ferns still hang in a neat row along the porch ceiling. Wide wooden planks stained gray and laid across the long porch are peeling and in need of repair.

Mason's mother, Hannah Hunter, follows the Feng Shui philosophy that red at the entrance of one's home brings good fortune and so refinished their front door with a bright-red wood stain. She transformed the family room of their historic home into her own personal workplace several years ago. From the outside, it seems that people come and go as they might in any shop. However, Mason's mother isn't a shopkeeper selling unique home goods or souvenirs like other businesses in Peaks Island.

Upon pushing down on the large, golden latch to open the creaky front door, a cold autumn wind blows leaves into the foyer. Mason can already hear faint chatter and chairs slowly scratching the kitchen floor as several people move trancelike into a standing position. He knows they must be in shock having just finished a session communicating with a deceased relative. Absolute absorption and a profound intensity begin to build in his head. He knows what comes next. The ghosts sense another medium and are trying to reach Mason. Swarms of different colors cloud his mind and charge at Mason with an intense energy that makes him feel light-headed as he angrily swats them away like hornets attacking. Mason slams the door behind him.

A voice from another room shouts, "Mason, you're home!"

Hannah appears in the foyer with her usual wool shawl (which Mason despises because it makes her look like a gypsy fortune-teller) draped over her shoulders. Mason continues to wave his arms in the air. Seeing his frustration during this supernatural experience, Hannah whispers in his ear, "It's a gift, Mason. Don't fight it, embrace it." In a normal tone, she asks, "How was school?"

"It's not a gift, it's a curse. I don't want to see ghosts. Everyone thinks we're weird."

"Mason, not now." Turning to her guests as they enter the foyer to join them, Hannah says, "Mason is going through a confusing time right now. Teenagers, you know?"

Mason rolls his eyes in response. He wants to say more but knows it's useless.

"I beat Jack again." Mason always shares his winning games with Hannah. What Mason doesn't share is *how* he wins. The memory of today's game flashes back to him.

Mason is sitting across from Sarah, who is all confidence. Her straight black hair frames big, round, brown eyes. Two girls stand beside her and motion to more friends to come over and watch the game. A couple of guys, including Trent, come over and gather around the chess set on the lunch table. Trent looks at Mason and makes ghostly gestures. He adds a ghostly "boooohhh" and laughs.

"Sarah, why are you playing with this loser?" Trent asks.

"It's for chess club, Trent. If I beat Mason Hunter, I can play in the championship next semester, and you know how top tier schools like that," Sarah says while examining the chessboard. She doesn't even look at Mason; it's like he isn't there at all.

Mason *is* there. He is there even if his classmates treat him like he is invisible. He wishes he could beat Sarah fair and square, but he knows he can't, and right now there are others standing next to Mason who really are invisible. People only Mason can see, and this is his secret weapon.

"Line up your rook to protect the queen," an old man only Mason can see says. Step-by-step, the old man guides Mason through the game until he makes a final move next to Sarah's king, and Mason says, "Checkmate."

Sarah's jaw drops. The crowd dissipates without saying a word. Only Mrs. Janet, the chess club coach, smiles wide and congratulates Mason. Mason shakes Mrs. Janet's hand and thanks her but can't seem to make eye contact, knowing he didn't win fairly.

Mason stormed out of the lunchroom and decided to cut class for the rest of the day. He kept thinking about Trent's obnoxious laugh and Sarah's indifference toward him. As much as he enjoyed seeing the shock on her face when he won, he couldn't revel in his win, knowing he cheated. If only senior year would end and he could leave this place. He hoped that he never saw any of them again. He spent the rest of his day at the port to watch the ferries before returning home.

Back at the Hunters' home, Hannah says, "I knew you would win." She turns over her shoulder to look at her guests and says, "Mason is brilliant at chess. He has what it takes to become a grandmaster like Bobby Fischer!"

"Who?" asks one of the guests.

"Bobby Fischer. He became the youngest grandmaster in the 1950s or '60s when he was only fifteen years old. Eventually, he became the World Chess Champion," Mason replies.

"Hmm," one woman replies with feigned interest.

In truth, Mason was not interested in pursuing a lifelong chess career like Bobby Fischer did because of the game itself. After all, Bobby Fischer was a paranoid eccentric who ended up living a reclusive life in Iceland. Some thought he was schizophrenic. Mason imagines a more exciting life for himself and knows that chess could be the means to the fame and fortune he longs for. He yearns for a life where he doesn't have to deal with people like Trent. The title of grandmaster is a title he wants to attain not because he loves chess but because of all the people he could impress with it. At the very least, it would be a bonus on a college application and good for bragging rights at some future cocktail party or other event.

The two middle-aged women standing in the foyer smile at Mason and then sheepishly hug Hannah. "Thank you. We will call you to set up the next, uh, session," one of them says.

They close the door, and Hannah says, "Let me clean up a bit. Apple slices? Or popcorn?"

"Both."

In the kitchen, Mason sits at the kitchen table and watches his mother add two tablespoons of ghee to a medium-sized pot and turn on the stove. She adds the popcorn kernels, closes the lid, and begins washing and peeling an apple. In a few minutes, the popcorn kernels start popping.

"Did Ms. Garrett sign the detention form?" Hannah asks as she walks toward the table with a plate of apple slices and a bowl of popcorn. She bends over and kisses Mason on the cheek, which he wipes off. He feels guilty for doing so, but ever since he was about twelve years old, physical affection from his mother suddenly felt repulsive. It's embarrassing and diminishes his perception of himself as a man. He was about to apologize, but Hannah pats Mason on the head before sitting down beside him. That made it so much worse.

The detention form for day 5 of detention was signed, and he had only three more days before being allowed regular lunch break. It had been six days since Mason was called into Principal Taylor's office and warned, "These kinds of physical outbursts will not be tolerated." How could Mason explain himself to Principal Taylor? Just the other day, Mason overheard the sophomore English teachers talking about how fit and well-dressed their principal is. One of them said she planned on baking her special cheesecake for their next meeting because she knows how much he likes it.

It began last week while Mason was bemused watching Bella read from her chemistry book. Out of nowhere, Trent Stellar came up from behind her, rubbed her back, and planted an unwanted kiss on her cheek. Mason saw the embarrassment in Bella's face. If he were braver, he would have said something to Trent right at that moment. Something like "Leave her alone, scumbag." He wanted to stand up to that bully, but he didn't. Instead, he lowered his head into his own book and pretended not to have seen anything. His shame and embarrassment for being such a coward stung.

Later that same day, Trent approached Mason by bumping shoulders with him in the hall and said, "Talk to any ghosts lately?"

That brought Mason to his breaking point, and he wanted so bad to hit him. Mason clenched his fists and rushed over to Trent. But when they stood face-to-face, he froze. Mason managed to open his mouth, but no words came out. Standing there, with his mouth open, face-to-face with Trent, Trent pushed him away. Mason fell backward just as a rush of students came out of a nearby classroom. One of them bumped into Trent, causing him to trip over Mason's backpack and fall on top of him. Mason pushed Trent off, and in the process, Trent hit the back of his head against the wall behind them. Principal Taylor only saw that last part and grabbed both boys under their arms and demanded they follow him to his office. Trent claimed that Mason pushed him first. Mason tried to deny it, but Principal Taylor said it didn't matter.

"Absolutely no violence is tolerated regardless of who started it. Mason, if not for your outstanding academic record and series of chess trophies for Port High School, you'd be expelled. Trent, you are lucky, and I mean lucky that I don't kick you off the lacrosse team for the rest of the year." Hence, both students were placed in detention as punishment.

His torment from Trent began back in the seventh grade. Many of the kids picked up from their parents that Hannah Mason worked as a medium. One warm September day that year, Trent and some other kids from school were at their local ice cream shop when Mason and Hannah walked in. The lady serving ice cream was always a source of wicked comedic relief for Trent and his friends due to her lazy eye, stuttering speech, and colorful hair accessories. When Mason and his mother approached the counter, she exclaimed, "Hannah!"

"Hi, Mary," Hannah replied, and Mason could quickly see his classmates coming closer to hear Mary stutter.

"I… I want to thank you for he-helping me visit with my d-d-d-dad."

The kids laughed, and Hannah gave them a stern look before replying, "I am happy to help, Mary."

Mason was mortified. Standing there before his peers, he knew for certain that he never wants to work as a medium. Mason stormed out of the ice cream store and in the process slipped on some melted ice cream on the floor. His humiliation was complete as Trent stood up laughing, bent over, and clutched his belly, and the rest of his crew joined in.

Now seventeen years old, Mason looks at himself in the mirror and is aware that he actually has become quite handsome despite the bullying he experiences. His face is oval with a well-defined jaw. He thinks about Brad Pitt and tries to draw comparisons. He examines his nose from the front and side, noting that it is long, straight, and slightly hawklike, giving him an intriguing fierceness. His hair is wavy, dark blond, and perfect for the popular undercut style he usually wears, but now it has grown long enough for him to tuck behind his ears. His almond-shaped dark-brown eyes are intense and gleam with the brilliance that lie behind them. The bullying at school would have been unbearable, but Mason has always found solace in his outstanding academic record and the ease with which he has always been able to grasp most school subjects.

Mason's greatest source of relief comes from James Villas, his childhood friend. James attends a private school, but the two met learning to play hockey in kindergarten. They continue to play on a house league. Occasionally, James invites Mason to hang out with some of his private school friends, who would be considered "nerdy" at Mason's school, but Mason finds them interesting and funny.

"Mason, that guy Trent is a complete jerk. I would just stay away. I mean high school will be over before we know it, anyway. We'll all be far away from here," James says as he tries to console Mason.

Mason nods and imagines a life somewhere far from Peaks Island where people didn't know Hannah is a medium. Somewhere where new friends wouldn't quietly disappear from Mason's life after receiving whispers about how weird Mason and his family are. Sometimes, an entire day at school would end with Mason not having said a single word to anyone. His day-to-day life is a quiet, internal experience of the books he reads and the occasional ghosts he is accustomed to seeing walking about. Hannah occasionally tries to get Mason to open up to her about his experiences with ghosts or life in general but to no avail. After all, Hannah is the cause of so much of the grief in his life.

"Mason, you have to understand that these people hurt each day and ache for the ones they lost. By reaching out to the other side, we can help all of them find peace. In turn, we increase the positive energy in our universe, enabling all beings to move freely into their destinies. We can help clear the way for new life."

Mason snickers and rolls his eyes again. Slowly, a ghostly figure floats up behind him. The ghost was a man in his forties. Hannah smiles at the man, but he looks at Mason. "I know you are there. Just go away before I turn the fan on, and you're blown away." He laughs.

"Mason!" Hannah yells. "Frank lost his family. They are in mourning and came today to say goodbye. How can you not feel for them!"

"So didn't they say goodbye already? Wasn't that the point of your little séance today? Please, go away, Frank. You don't belong in this house. Not now, not ever!" And as the anger rises within Mason, energy exudes from him that pushes the ghostly figure back into oblivion.

CHAPTER 2

WESLEY

There is a supernatural force within the workings of love that none of us, not even scientists, can deny.

—Ken Poirot

U p the wooden staircase and down a short narrow hallway, Mason's bedroom door opens to dark-gray tones and contemporary decor apart from an old desk Hannah said was passed down for generations of Hunters. Mason always loved the desk with its thick legs resembling tree trunks and asked to keep it in his room. The desk was carved to look like the bark of a tree, and the desktop's grain was detailed and rich in color. The best part is the chessboard inlaid on the desktop. Mason's admiration for it gave him a strong desire to have it close to him.

Mason lay on the striped navy-blue-and-gray comforter on his bed. He opens his laptop and searches YouTube. Lately, he is enamored with Cage the Elephant's "Cold Cold Cold." While listening to singer Matt Shultz plead out the lyrics, Mason scans each book on his shelf with his eyes, including, *To Kill a Mockingbird, A Farewell to Arms, The Things They Carried,* and his current book, *Fahrenheit 451.* He contemplates picking it up but feels distracted. Mason can't seem to focus enough to read or do his endless homework.

Looking around his room, he sees his hockey jersey hanging out of the hamper and makes a mental note to throw it in the wash before his next game on Saturday. Hockey is Mason's best outlet from the ghosts in his home and the daily torment he feels at school. There is no replacement for the adrenaline rush he feels as he races to get to the flying puck before his opponent. He lets his mind drift into a daydream of winning the Stanley Cup and imagines the fame and fortune that would naturally follow even though he plays on a house league and never even made it to a competitive travel team.

Revved up by his daydream, Mason gets down on the ground and begins doing push-ups. His routine is ten push-ups, hold plank position for thirty seconds, and then mountain climbers for thirty seconds. He repeats this as many times as he could. Standing up, he looks at his arms in the mirror, noting some increased definition in the past few months.

Suddenly, Mason hears a Zippo lighter flick open, and the glow of a cigarette appears. Sitting at Mason's heavy desk is a man in his midforties. He is a large man with full lips and shining brown eyes.

With a heavy Southern accent, the spirit's introduction comes out slow and drawn out. "Aahm Wesley. Aahm here to help you, boy."

He takes a drag of his cigarette and stands up. Mason notices that the man is wearing a dark-gray pin-striped suit in the fashion of a Southern gentleman. The gold chain of a pocket watch is hanging elegantly from his trousers.

"Where did you come from?" Mason asks.

"Same place as awll of your uninvited guests. But aahm not heeah because your mama summoned me, boy. Aahm heeah fow you and aah have waited a looong time fow ma prodigy to come of age. An' now, well, heeah we both awe, of sound body and mind!"

He lets out a roaring laugh as he lays his left hand on his heaving belly. This figure, which doesn't look like a ghost but a real man, has the strongest supernatural presence that Mason has ever felt. A force to be reckoned with, for sure, but whether or not that force is for good or evil, Mason can't tell. Nonetheless, at this first introduction, he is intrigued.

"There is so much aah need to show you." Wesley puts his hand on Mason's shoulder, and suddenly the two of them are transported to a different place and time. Mason finds himself surrounded by breathtaking oak trees. Some of their thick branches curve upward toward the blue sky and others extend outward. Moss hangs from the branches so low it nearly dips into the most reflective pond Mason has ever seen. The surface of the pond is an exact replica of the colorful azaleas, daffodils, and camellias growing all around.

"Welcome to Charleston, South Carolina. This is the planta-tion where aah was born and raised. Life in South Carolina in the 1920s was rough. In 1921, the boll weevil migration to the cotton fields of South Carolina from Mexico wiped out the sea island cotton crop. We endured years of drought. Farmlands had lost half their value, and one third of the state's farms were mortgaged.

"Aah was only twenty-one years old then, just a few years older than you, and next in line, after my older brother William, to inherit the plantation. The previous year, our father caught malaria and passed on. William took control of the plantation with his pretty new bride, Grace. That summer, Grace's cousin, Charlotte, from Boston came to stay with us. One look at her and aah was in love. The first evening of her stay, Charlotte sang for us. Boy, this girl sang like a nightingale. Aah swore to myself that aah would not go a single day on this earth without hearing that voice, so help me God.

"Charlotte and aah would stroll through the gardens on the plantation most afternoons. Those are my most cherished memories. One particular such day, Charlotte wore the most exquisite green dress that brought out the green in her greenish blue eyes. We walked on the dirt path along the pond, with bright camellias occasionally brushing our necks and yellah daffodils up to our knees.

"She told me how she loved the movies and wanted nothing more than to be a famous Hollywood actress. Whenever and as often as she could, Charlotte would go to the movies. Sometimes, we went together. Her favorite was The Queen of Sheba, a silent film about the ill-fated romance between Solomon, King of Israel, and the Queen of Sheba. Charlotte loved the lavish costumes and performances by Betty Blythe and Fritz Leiber. Aah loved when Charlotte would reenact scenes from the film with over-the-top drama, often falling into my arms as aah caught her after a near miss."

Mason listens carefully as the large Southern gentleman rambles on about his life. Mason knows that this story will have some tragic ending, otherwise, this soul would be resting peacefully. Mason considers ending this charade as he had heard at least a dozen of these tales…although this was the first time a spirit made first contact entirely on its own, rather than having been summoned by Hannah via request of the deceased's family. This spirit had been dead a long time and was not one of those recently departed. Plus, Mason had never been transported anywhere by a ghost. How was this possible? No one in his family had ever described traveling to a different time and place via a ghost. Why is this happening, and why did this ghost choose Mason?

Wesley continues with his story. "It was one autumn eve-ning that would change our lives forever. The day was unusually hot for that time of year as it must have been over ninety-five degrees. After dinner, Charlotte and aah thought we might catch a breeze on a late-night stroll. As we walked, we heard music coming from somewhere far off. We listened carefully and picked up the sounds of guitar, saxophone, and drums… it was jazz. We had heard it be-fo-wah, but as we followed the music, we heard people too. They were dancing what today y'all call the Charleston. The Charleston had only recently gained some popularity here in South Carolina, although most places banned it.

"We walked up to the slaves' cabin located in the south-east end of the plantation, opened the door, and walked inside. The music stopped when they saw us, but Charlotte started to hum, tap her feet, and dance without music. Aah stood there, motionless, speechless. The drummer started to play and each musician, after seeing that aah did not object, also began to play. In a minute, everyone was in full swing again. Charlotte pulled me close and said, 'It's four basic steps, arms swinging loosely in the opposite direction of the legs. This is amazing!' She smiled, and aah couldn't resist joining her in this uninhibited dance.

"The next morning over breakfast, Charlotte oozed excite-ment as she described the evening in detail to Grace and William. 'I never felt so alive! The music was incredible, it was like the drums were beating in my chest…' Grace, looking shocked, snapped out of her frozen state and interrupted Charlotte, 'Wait, are you telling me you were inside the slaves' cabins, dancing? Wesley, you allowed this? Do you know how bad this makes us look?' William added, 'Aah don't believe this, Wesley. How are we supposed to run a plantation if we are dancing with our own field hands!' Charlotte and aah followed William as he stormed angrily around the corner into his office." William slammed his hand on the wooden desk in front of him.

Mason has been watching this story unfold with Wesley beside him relaying occasional bits and pieces of information. But now, Mason's focus shifts to the same desk William's hand has come down hard on. He recognizes that wood grain, and as his eyes travel around and down the side of the desk, the legs are unmistakably the same as those of the desk in Mason's bedroom. Wesley notices Mason's realization and states, "It's the same desk, an antique now."

"But I don't understand, how did your desk end up in my room? Is that what brought you here?" Mason asks.

"Heavens no. The desk did not bring me to you. Aah made sure the desk would end up in good hands. Aah chose you not just to be the owner of the beloved desk my father built but for what you must do. That which aah was unable to complete in my life."

"I don't understand," Mason says the words slowly with an obvious tone of annoyance.

"Patience, Mason. You will see and you will understand," Wesley replies.

Wesley continues with his tale. "Irritated, Charlotte told William and Grace that she could never live the way they do, with their rigid rules, orders, and obligations. William explained that she was too young and apparently too naive to understand what it means to be an adult with responsibilities. 'If y'all lived as free as y'all would like, there'd be no plantation or money to buy y'all fancy dresses and tickets to movies and trips to all parts of the country in the finest trains,' he said.

"As the argument heated, Charlotte stormed out, and aah headed out after her. When we were finally alone, we were sitting on her silken chase lounge. She was upset and more beautiful than ever. With the sunlight coming in through the window and her eyes glistening, aah leaned in and kissed her, slowly. Her anger had made her lips unusually warm, and aah placed my hand above her chest. It was so warm, and aah could feel her every breath…steady and then intensify slightly. Charlotte wasn't shy, not ever. As she pulled away from our kiss, Charlotte looked in my eyes, and aah swear she could see right into my soul. With the most serious expression, she said, 'Let's leave together. We do not belong at this plantation.'

"After a long discussion with William and Grace, they agreed that Charlotte and aah travel together to Boston, Massachusetts, with one condition: that we travel as a couple, engaged to be married. In those years, a young woman's reputation and prospects for marrying well would be greatly diminished if it became known that she traveled with a man not her relative or fiancé, or husband, and her virtue questioned. William had already given Grace our mother's engagement ring, but there was another ring in our mother's jewelry box with an onyx stone set in a platinum band with small diamond surrounding it."

Mason looks on as a young Wesley presents the ring to Charlotte, and then says, "It's like the night sky that goes on forever, like my love for you. Marry me, Charlotte." Charlotte smiles and says yes as Wesley slides the ring on her slender finger.

"We traveled by train to Boston. Diesel trains didn't make it to America from Europe until the 1930s, so we were fortunate to have lived during the era of steam locomotives. Although employees of the railroad companies were on strike quite often for higher wages at that time, the steam trains themselves were quite an experience. The South was known fo-wah having the most beautiful depots and railroad facilities. George Pullman was an acquaintance of mine and made sure Charlotte and I were given an exclusive tour of the parlor, diner, and best sleepers his Pullman Palace Car Company built for the train.

"We stood on the platform waiting for the train as its cylinder and piston cranked loudly to a full stop. Smoke pumped out from the chimney and floated like shadows all around us. A hot breeze from the smokestack blew past, bringing with it a smell of metal and coal so sharp you could almost taste it. Charlotte stood quietly, holding a handkerchief to her mouth. We stepped onto the train along with at least fifty other passengers, found our red velvet covered seats and soon heard the *chuga, chuga, chuga, chuga, chug* of the engines pushing the train onward. The experience of crossing trestles and going through tunnels just to emerge out to a glorious countryside felt like defying gravity and time. It was autumn, and the weather had finally cooled. The trees presented a firestorm of colors, and I noticed Charlotte watching the scene go by. Her large eyes reminded me of a deer seeking shelter near a lake when a forest is ablaze.

"It was on the train to Boston that we met Adrian Blake. Adrian appeared to be the most quintessential 1920s gentleman. Clean-shaven with a homburg hat, dark wool suit with her-ringbone pattern, and two-tone Oxford shoes. He was in his late twenties then, and aah must admit, he had a smile that shone a mile away, especially when he first laid his eyes on Charlotte.

"'Pardon me, sir. Are the two of you staying in Chicago?' Adrian asked as the train rattled along.

"'One day to see Chicago and one night at the Palmer House. From there 'tis onward to Boston,' aah replied.

"'Boston! My, that is where I am headed. I have an idea for a new movie but need the right leading lady." With that, Adrian turned and smiled at Charlotte.

"Her eyes lit up as she gently touched my elbow but leaned in toward Adrian with the next bump of the train on its tracks. 'What's the movie about?' she inquired.

"Adrian told us about his big idea fo-wah a movie. It was a story set in a small town about a beautiful ballet dancer who falls fo-wah her dance instructor but gets sidetracked by some mischievous other dancers in the group. Eventually, she finds her strength and leaves alone fo-wah New York City where she becomes a famous dancer.

"When we arrived at the Palmer House in Chicago, aah was in awe of the majestic beauty of the place. Incredibly high and intricately painted ceilings soared above various well-dressed people. There were winged statue candelabras taller than myself. Don't forget, at that time, aah hadn't traveled that far away from Charleston, and Chicago was very different. It was bigger, faster, and so alive.

"An attractive lady around twenty-five years of age came up to Charlotte in the hotel lobby and complimented her scarf. She was slender with blond hair and hazel eyes. She reminded me of a picture of a French lady aah had seen as a boy. Her eyebrows so perfectly arched they might as well have been drawn by hand. Her high cheekbones sat on either side of her small upturned nose. Her coat and hat were burgundy, and her gloves and scarf deep purple. For some reason, aah still remember the pin in her coat lapel. It was a dragonfly with ruby stones. She turned toward Charlotte and enthusiastically exclaimed 'That emerald-green color is very becoming on you! Isn't the Palmer House just divine? Is this your first time in Chicago?'

"'Yes, it is. I'm Charlotte," she replies with an outstretched hand. The two women look pretty as they stand side by side. Farah, a classic beauty, and my Charlotte, her fiery green eyes giving away her adventurous spirit, try as she might to play the part of a Southern damsel.

"'Hi, Charlotte, I'm Farah. Have you heard that the World's Fair will return to Chicago in April of 1925?'

"'No, I haven't. I remember some talk between my parents and their friends about the last World's Fair. I think it was in 1892 or 1893…'

"'Well, this time, they are going to call it the Women's World Fair to celebrate our right to vote and how different the world has become for women. I was just a little girl then, but I still remember going with my family on July 4, and there were absolutely no female speakers. The world is changing, thank goodness. I would like to become involved in the planning and organizing of our Women's Fair, and you have to come back for it!'

"'It sounds fantastic. Actually, I came here with my friends, and we are planning on making a movie about a dancer who moves to New York…but maybe we can change the set to Chicago during the fair. I'm sure it will make for a beautiful backdrop.'

"'A movie! Wow, that's incredible. I love movies.'

"That's how the friendship between Charlotte and Farah began."

Suddenly, Mason hears a knock on a door and Hannah's voice. "Mason?" With that, Mason is immediately transported back to his bedroom as if nothing had happened.

"Yes, Mom?" he replies.

"What do you feel like having for dinner? I didn't get a chance to make anything tonight, so we can order something for delivery, or I can pick it up. Italian?"

Not mentioning anything he had seen and trying to look as normal as possible, Mason thinks for a second about what he wanted to eat. "Let's go Greek tonight. I'm craving Avgolemono soup and grilled octopus."

"Perfect. Should I add an order of lamb chops?" Hannah asks.

"Sounds good, Mom," Mason replies as Hannah smiled and walked out of the room. Mason waits a minute before getting up to close the door again. The moment he turns around, he is back at the Palmer House with Wesley, watching like a ghost as Wesley continues to narrate his story.

"Charlotte and aah were wed on a picturesque snowy January day in Boston in 1924. The event was spectacular, and Charlotte looked more dazzling than evah. Her wedding headpiece had diamonds that covered half her head, and her bouquet dripped down to the flo-wah. William and Grace rode the train in from South Carolina, along with a few aunts, uncles, and cousins. Grace said that she had never felt cold like winter in Boston befo-wah and couldn't find anything warm enough to wear in the stores in Charleston. While the Southerners complained about the cold, they were few as most of our guests were Charlotte's friends and family who lived nearby. Nonetheless, it was obvious to see who was from the south and who was from the north as us Southerners prefer to wear lighter colors while the northerners prefer deeper tones, and their women all had their hands in fur muffs to keep warm.

"The Vine Mansion where we celebrated our wedding was decorated with enormous ice sculptures and fountains of champagne poured in pyramids of champagne flutes. The chandeliers sparkled, and our guests seemed to share our excitement. All in all, we had around one hundred guests or so. The music was fast and loud. We all danced the Charleston to a live band. Charlotte, Farah, Lillian Tolbert, Adrian, and aah must have danced fo-wah hours before the final guest left. The five of us remained at the end, and instead of a wedding night alone with my wife, we were laughing and drinking before passing out upstairs in one of the mansion's great rooms.

"Everywhere we went, it seemed that the universe was conspiring to help Charlotte succeed. Meeting Adrian on the train, arriving in Chicago, meeting Farah, the Women's Fair, it was all in her favor. We continued on to Boston, but the ladies kept in touch and would later work together not only in planning the Women's World Fair, but Adrian agreed to give Farah a small part in his movie. In Adrian's movie, Farah played one of the mischievous dancers who took Charlotte's character out fo-wah too many drinks the night before a big audition, causing that character to almost fail the audition.

"Aah still remember the ladies' excitement years later at the Women's Fair, on April 18, 1925, when they heard Lillian give her speech. Ms. Tolbert was a big hit. She was a black inventor who devised a new kind of pitcher that kept ice separate in the core to keep drinks cold, called the Tolbert Pitcher. Ms. Tolbert beamed as she explained that the only man who had anything to do with her invention was the attorney at the patent office. Charlotte and Farah began discussing the possibility that a movie could be written, directed, and produced entirely by women. Aah thought it was cute. The three ladies became very good friends and quite an attractive threesome walking into several parties at the most coveted bars and restaurants of our time.

"Aah financed Adrian's first movie production, in its entirety. And the movie, which Adrian titled simply, *Born to Dance*, did rather well at the box office. More importantly, it skyrocketed me into the world of movie production. Adrian came up with several more film ideas and wanted Charlotte to star in them. Aah financed two more of Adrian's films, but other movie writers began sending me scripts. Better scripts. It broke my heart to turn down Adrian's next script, and it upset Charlotte quite a bit, seeing that the two had become quite accustomed to working together. That, plus Charlotte felt we owed Adrian some kind of loyalty. As far as aah was concerned, it was time to move on from Adrian. Our initial meeting on the train turned out to be fo-wah our mutual benefit. Adrian could not have gotten his first script to the big screen without me, and aah got my first start in the movie business. That's all.

"During that time, Charlotte and aah quarreled quite often, usually because Adrian was constantly discussing his ideas with her, but then when he presented them to me, aah had to turn them down. Charlotte was smitten with him. The way Adrian became overly excited about each film idea and his description of the role he created in each one especially fo-wah her. Aah overheard them discussing work more than once and, combined with a Gin Rickey, or two, it was just bad fo-wah business. Slowly, Adrian's drinking got out of hand. It was a shame to see a man fall so hard. He stopped writing scripts, and we began to see less and less of him.

"Aah produced and directed multiple films Charlotte starred in. She became quite famous. A few months after filming her fifth film, Charlotte became pregnant. We welcomed our daughter, Clara. She had beautiful gray-blue eyes and her mother's reddish-blond hair. Charlotte spent as much time as she could with Clara her first year and then began preparing fo-wah our next film. We were busy all day every day. It was difficult fo-wah us leaving Clara with a nanny so often those days, but Charlotte was worried that she would not be able to revive her career after having a baby if she waited too long.

"Unfortunately, Charlotte was never able to complete filming. On July 3, 1925, Charlotte and aah, along with Lillian and Farah with their dates, went to the Pickwick Club, a speakeasy, at Six Beach Street in downtown Boston. Even Adrian was there and congratulated us on the birth of our baby. We hugged and let bygones be bygones. Around 3:00 a.m. of July 4, there were still over one hundred people at the Pickwick. McGlennon's jazz orchestra was on the bandstand. Aah can still hear Johnny Duffy singing 'Twelfth Street Rag.' People were out on the flo-wah dancing and having a great time. Adrian pulled me outside to discuss his next idea fo-wah a movie away from the loud music.

"We stood outside smoking a cigar while Adrian shared with me his idea about two friends who become real estate tycoons and relocate to Florida where they build massive mansions and live lavish lifestyles until they fall in love with the same woman. Ultimately, the two men almost destroy everything they built together before they realize the woman was playing both of them.

"Adrian was completely immersed in telling the story when we heard the strangest sound, like a bag of sugar falling on paper. People started yelling from inside the club. Adrian and aah ran in but plaster was falling over our heads…"

"Mason! Dinner's here!" Hannah shouts from the bottom of the stairs of their home.

The Pickwick Club disappears, and Mason is once again in his room. He hurries downstairs to help Hannah set the table. Mason decides he did not want to share any of his experience with Wesley, in case Hannah overreacted and made much ado about nothing. So as he sits there eating his soup, Hannah asks him about his homework and if he had any big school projects coming up. They discuss their weekend plans, and Mason says that he would go see a movie with James and a few other guys from the hockey team.

Hannah reminds Mason that if he ever needed a way out of a difficult situation with his friends, to text her their code phrase: "Did you remember to feed Belle?" That is the name of their pet parrot and signals for Hannah to go pick up Mason. It was Hannah's way of protecting Mason from underage drinking or drugs. If Mason feels pressured to do something he knew he shouldn't, he would text the code phrase to Hannah to alert her of the situation. To date, Mason hasn't used the code.

When dinner is over, Mason tells Hannah that he had a few more chapters to read for history class and went back upstairs. As if he hasn't missed a beat, Wesley reappears in Mason's room and transports them back to the Pickwick Club. He continued his story.

"Adrian ran ahead into the club, but aah couldn't get in, and after a few minutes of trying to make my way through the people and falling plaster, the ceiling collapsed, the floor gave way, and two sidewalls caved in. Aah barely made it back outside when the whole building came crashing down. Aah panicked and prayed in frozen fear that Charlotte made it out from a back door somehow, but aah never saw her again. Charlotte and Adrian were among the forty-four people who died that night. The lead singer, Johnny Duffy, died too, leaving behind two little daughters of his own.

"The City of Boston blamed the collapse on the rigorous dancing and banned the Charleston dance rather than looking at the structural integrity of the building or occupancy levels. It took some time before it was revealed that a fire had occurred three months before and badly damaged the floors above the club. The building should never have reopened after the fire. Rainwater pooled on the roof, and the building collapsed. The city employees involved were indicted on various charges, but all were acquitted.

"Clara was only eighteen months old when her mamma passed. She has no recollection of her and knows her only from the movies she starred in. Clara watched those films over and over again as a little girl. In my grief, aah took Clara on a ferry ride where we could be on the water, away from the world. The ferryboat stopped at Peaks Island. Aah raised Clara, your great-grandmother, right here in this house."

Mason was stunned. It was quite an incredible story revealing that Charlotte's daughter was his great-grandmother. So Wesley was his great-great-grandfather? It was a lot to take in, and Mason realized that Hannah had never told him much about their family history other than that their family had been in Peaks Island and the East Coast for decades. Hannah was an only child of a couple who tried for many years to conceive a child and claimed it was a miracle when Hannah was born to her mother at age forty-five. Mason remembered his grandparents but did not know much about family members who lived before they did.

"Aah have plans fo-wah a new movie, Mason. Aah have big dreams fo-wah you."

"Why do you want to help me, Wesley? Why aren't you resting peacefully in the ever after? Your story was sad, but you made a mistake in choosing me. Hannah is the one who tries to help souls with unfinished business. I am not interested in hanging out with the dead. My mom is the one you should talk to. Thanks, but no thanks."

"That's why aah want you, Mason. It's that fire you have inside. Hannah is soft and sweet, not movie director material."

"Wait, so you want me to be a movie director? Oh my god!" Mason starts laughing. "I can't believe this. I can't believe I am talking with a ghost who wants to turn me into a movie director, and I haven't even graduated high school yet."

Wesley went on, "Look here now, you think you want to be an author, right? Well, many people do too but very, and I mean very, few people actually succeed in getting a book published and actually make a living off of writing books. You have a creative mind and can imagine all kinds of stories…you need to use that creativity and channel it into making movies. That's where the fame and fortune lies."

Mason is excited by the idea of being a famous movie director. Flashes of himself as a famous, adored, and envied movie director enter his mind, and he revels in the daydream for a few seconds, but he is quickly pulled back into the reality that he is still in his own bedroom and, what's worse, he is talking to a ghost. Maybe he is a freak after all. Mason decides he had had enough of this craziness.

"Let me show you…" Wesley begins to explain, but Mason yells, "Enough!" And with that, he lets his anger build up inside him. With the energy from his anger, Mason raises his hand and makes a pushing motion. Wesley falls backward and disappears.

Alone in his room again, Mason feels a quiet unease and then like something is crawling on his skin. It is the feeling of shame and disappointment. Mason has always envisioned himself as someone famous. If he were famous, he would be able to prove himself as someone to admire, rather than someone to taunt. But trying to achieve fame as a movie director via a ghost's advice just confirmed his weirdness. He turns his attention back to YouTube. He types in "I've Got No Roots," and Alice Merton's music video pops up. As the music begins, he raises the volume and dives into the images on the screen, trying to forget about Wesley, Charlotte, and the entire story he had heard only minutes before.

CHAPTER 3

VERSUS

*People understand me so poorly that they don't
even understand my complaint about them not
understanding me.*

—Søren Kierkegaard, *The
Journals of Kierkegaard*

The next day, Mason comes down for breakfast in his favorite H&M sweatshirt and jeans. Hannah is scrambling eggs, frying bacon, and cutting up some cantaloupe. Mason always looks forward to these big breakfasts. He has a sip of his mom's coffee and internally debates telling her about Wesley but decides he doesn't want to get into it. He figures Hannah would want to summon Wesley's spirit back, and Mason really didn't care to see him again.

"Good morning, Mason." His mom hugs him tight, and he squeezes her back. She smiles widely. "I'm so proud of you,

Mason." She holds a letter in her hand. "This $25,000 academic scholarship to Boston University is such a tremendous accomplishment."

Mason looks down and then lifts his gaze to meet Hannah's. He pauses a few moments before replying, "Mom, you know I don't want to go to Boston University. I want something else, something different."

Frustrated, Hannah answers her son sternly, "Mason, you don't know what you're talking about. Life isn't a game. You can't turn down a scholarship because you want to do something else but don't know what that something else is. You can't just throw it away! You're not making any sense!"

Mason rises from his chair, pushing it backward that it almost falls, and storms out of the kitchen. Sitting alone in his room, he recalls how sad and defeated his mother always appeared when she had to pick up Mason from the school for fighting with other kids. Mason put his mother through a lot, but this is *his* life, and he can't let his guilt get in the way of his goals. He can't just do what Hannah wants to appease her for the burden of raising him as a single mom.

When Mason was a little boy, his days were filled with days at the beach, nights catching fireflies, and finger painting with his grandparents who lived with him in the house on Peaks Island. But when they died, Mason was suddenly alone with his mom in a town where many people considered Hannah an outcast because of her work as a medium. When his grandparents were alive, Mason always felt he had their support and protection. They were well respected with the neighbors and would never allow anyone to speak negatively of Mason or Hannah. In particular, Mason's grandmother was known to have a sharp tongue and never hesitated to tell someone to mind their own business when they inquired in a negative way about Hannah being a medium, and her quiet, oddly serious son.

One day, when Mason was about nine years old, their neighbor, Ms. Langely, was trimming her boxwood bushes. When she saw Mason's grandmother sitting in the backyard with her usual afternoon iced tea, she walked over still wearing her wide brimmed hat and gardening gloves and asked, "Honey, what is going on with all those people coming and going from your place lately?"

Knowing that Ms. Langely had a penchant for gossip, Mason's grandmother replied, "Ms. Langely, such a hot day today, isn't it? Come here and have a glass of iced tea with me. Rumor has it that you are no longer interested in being the town gossip."

Ms. Langely's jaw dropped, and she walked away in a huff. But now, Mason's grandparents were gone, and Mason felt the town's eyes and talk around him everywhere he went.

Then there was also Anthony Villas, James's father. The friendship between Anthony and Hannah began to develop when Mason and James were only four years old. Their relationship slowly grew over afternoons watching the kids play hockey. Anthony would always bring Hannah a hot coffee and sit beside her as they cheered their kids on. He was warm and understanding toward Hannah because he could relate to being a single parent. Anthony became a father in his midtwenties when his girlfriend unexpectedly became pregnant with James. They knew the relationship was not meant to last and decided to share custody of their son.

Mason always cringed when he saw how Hannah smiled in Anthony's presence. He could tell his mother was attracted to Anthony's rugged appearance. His hair was dark and wavy, and he always had a bit of facial hair. Anthony always smiled when he looked at Hannah, and it was genuine and bright. His eyes were a light brown but looked hazel in the sunlight. A regular at the gym, Anthony had a muscular physique. He was intelligent, giving, and not arrogant in the least. He seemed perfect…a perfect threat to Mason. The idea of his mother with his best friend's father was unnerving. More than once, Mason missed a shot on the ice because he was too distracted trying to catch a glimpse of how Hannah was behaving with Anthony.

Mason didn't discuss his agitation about Anthony with James. He and Mason played hockey together since they were toddlers and were more like brothers than friends. Oddly, the two boys always looked like brothers too. They had the same hair and eye color, but James was just an inch or so taller than Mason. Unlike Mason, James was always popular with the kids at his school.

One evening when Mason was about twelve years old, Hannah came to pick up Mason from the Villas' home. He heard Anthony invite Hannah in for a cup of tea. Mason listened in while James finished playing a video game. Anthony talked about how he moved to New York after college, but when his father fell ill, he returned home to Maine to help his parents.

"I have an idea I'd like to share with you. I see plastic cups all over the beach, and as you know, I grew up beside the beach in Maine and have loved the ocean my entire life. Every time I go to the grocery store and see all the plastic bags being used to pack food, all I could think about is how much of it will end up in the ocean. I can't pick up a plastic fork at a fast food restaurant anymore without thinking that I am holding a meaningless and wasteful object that never disintegrates. I have been saving money for years but need more to accomplish what I want. Do you think you'd be interested in organizing and hosting fundraisers for me? I think you'd be great at it, and I would be forever in your debt."

Over the next two years, Hannah helped coordinate many of those fundraising events. Eventually, Anthony opened a small grocery store concept where absolutely no plastic or waste is created. Together with a friend of a friend who owned a farm, they produced all their own produce, meat, and dairy and sold it at the store. There was no plastic used. Everything was transported with reusable crates. The store sold canvas tote bags and glass containers that customers were urged to bring back and reuse.

The first store was a huge success, and Anthony opened several more stores in the East Coast.

One year ago, Anthony was approached by a representative of a chain grocery store who offered him a massive sum of money to use the store's name, "Tony's," and turn his concept into a nationwide chain. Anthony agreed and since then has slowly amassed a small fortune.

Mason was bewildered by the fact that despite his financial success, Anthony chose to live rather simply. He didn't move out of town but bought a new house for himself with a bedroom for James that was only slightly larger and nicer than his previous one. He chose a newer version of his Jeep Wrangler with some extra features, but other than that, he spent a lot of his free time at his stores, charity functions, and hockey games with James, Mason, and Hannah. Mason imagined the glamorous car, home, and toys he would buy if he had the kind of money that Anthony has.

Mason was well aware that Hannah admires Anthony's humility, but Mason found that aspect of his personality underwhelming.

"James, why doesn't your dad move you out of this boring town and into some Beverly Hills mansion? You know he has the money to do it."

Mason knew that James was always protective of Mason's feelings, and this made James feel more like a brother to him. The fact that Mason was very sensitive to the idea of his mom with Anthony was mutually understood by both Mason and

James, without Mason ever having to come right out and say it. They both knew that Anthony stayed in Portland to be close to Hannah, and Mason anticipated James's feigned ignorance when he shrugged and said, "Right? I'll never understand the man."

*****

The two of them glide on the ice naturally and hit shot after shot to victory with their team. It was nearing the end of the season, and their coach invite all the players and their parents to meet after the game at Salvage BBQ on Congress Street in Portland, Maine.

While sitting with his teammates, Mason can still catch pieces of Anthony and Hannah's conversation. Anthony is thanking Hannah for helping him in the early days of Tony's whenever there were hiccups. Something about a power outage and the backup generator malfunctioning. "Not only did you help clean out the refrigerators, you offered me a loan to pay for the damage. Even though I couldn't accept your money, Hannah, I want you to know that your offer meant the world to me back then and still does today."

Mason doesn't know any of that had happened. How could Hannah have offered Anthony a loan when she keeps pressuring Mason to get good grades for a scholarship? Does Anthony mean that much to her? Does he mean more to her than Mason does?

It is time that he interrupts the conversation. Leaning over the table to talk to Anthony, Mason says, "The other day, I came home from school and my mom was just finishing up a séance. You know she works as a medium, right?"

James nudges him to quit, but Mason knows that Hannah's work as a medium is often the elephant in the room because Anthony is aware that Hannah works as a medium and finds it very strange. From what James had told him, it is not a part of Hannah's life that Anthony particularly likes but is able to push it aside and focus on the many things he does like about her.

"Yes, I know that, Mason."

"Mason, you know I help people find closure when they lost someone close to them. Don't talk about my work like it's something shameful. By looking at photos of their departed ones and talking to them about the person a little, I can help ease the pain of their loved ones' parting," she explains.

"So, do you actually see the ghosts?" Anthony asks.

Hannah senses his disbelief and lies, "No, I just try and talk to them more like a psychologist would and assure them that their loved ones are in a better place and at peace."

Hannah throws Mason a disapproving "we'll talk about this later" kind of look.

Anthony turns toward Hannah so Mason and James can't hear him and quickly changes the subject. "James is asking to go to Lollapalooza in Chicago this summer...if Mason hasn't brought it up yet, I'm guessing he is still just buttering you up."

"No buttering up is happening yet, but I'll be looking forward to it," Hannah replies.

The music in the restaurant changes, and Mason cringes at the sight of Hannah and Anthony smiling at each other. "Let It Happen" by Tame Impala comes on, and Hannah starts singing along. Anthony joins in on the singing, and the hockey team erupts in laughter. Some of them hide their heads and others pretend to throw things at them to stop singing.

"We're such rock stars, Tony. Looks like our boys might have two parent chaperones at Lollapalooza," Hannah whispers to Anthony.

James's mother remarried when James was still a baby, and he was accustomed to spending days with his mother, stepfather, and stepsister. When it was Anthony's turn to have James at his house, James immediately felt the quiet loneliness in his father's house and worried that his dad would never meet anyone. But for Mason, it was different.

Mason did not have the same hope as James of seeing his parent in a new relationship. Hannah and Mason lived with Hannah's parents after Mason was born, but they were already much older and passed away just months apart when Mason was ten years old. Mason was particularly close to his grandfather and cherished days spent with him reading books and playing card games like Old Maid and Go Fish. As his only father figure, his grandfather's passing was very difficult for Mason and left a void he couldn't fill. For a few months after his grandfather's death, Mason was able to recall the peculiar smell of his sweater, a combination of dryer sheets and aftershave. He always hid mints in his sweater pockets for Mason to find. But slowly, Mason's memories of his grandparents started to fade.

Just a few days after his grandfather died, Mason came home from school to find Anthony consoling Hannah in an intimate embrace in the kitchen. Mason felt betrayed, became furious, and threw his schoolbag at Anthony. He realized that they were more than just friends, and the new image of his mother with James's father was overwhelming. Hannah tried explaining the importance of grown-ups having meaningful relationships with other grown-ups, but Mason couldn't understand. Soon after that, Mason started acting up aggressively toward other kids in school, so Hannah decided to wait until he was older to date openly.

After lunch at Salvage BBQ, the hockey players and their parents walk out to the parking lot.

Hannah walks up to her car and immediately notices a flat tire. "Mason, we have flat," she says, looking at her son. Every once in a while, Mason still smiled at his mother the way he did when he was a small child, an image Hannah cherished. He smiles at her that way now.

"Lucky for you your son is a handy mechanic." Mason opens the trunk, takes out his tools, and pulls out the spare. James and Anthony walk up to them.

"That sucks. Let me help," James says.

While the two of them work together on the flat, Anthony turns to Hannah, out of earshot of their sons. "There is this great Korean restaurant that just opened in town. It has traditional Korean food, great kimchi. Do you want to go?"

Smiling, Hannah says, "That would be great. Friday night?"

Looking over his shoulder to make sure Mason couldn't hear, Anthony leans a bit into Hannah and whispers, "It's a date."

While Hannah and Tony are talking, James turns to Mason. "What was with that talking to ghost stuff back there? Have you asked your mom about Lollapalooza yet? You're supposed to be on good terms with her, remember?"

"I'll ask her later, I'm not worried about it," Mason replies. But he is worried. He really wants to go and doesn't want to be the kid who doesn't go because his mom wouldn't let him. Hannah is really weird about Mason staying anywhere overnight without her. What are the chances she is going to let him go to Chicago with James? Now he regretted that comment he made about Hannah's séance.

Back home, Mason watches as Hannah pours herself one of her favorite cabernet sauvignon wines, Meiomi, and turns on her Sonos speaker to Pandora. "Dog Days Are Over" by Florence and the Machine comes on. He waits until she drinks a full glass and seems to have mellowed out. He thinks it would be a good time to bring up Lollapalooza, but Hannah starts talking first, and it isn't what he wants to hear.

"Mason, I didn't like how you acted at Salvage BBQ earlier. You were disrespectful to me. Why would you want to embarrass me like that?"

Crap. Not the conversation he wants to have, and he knows he should just apologize so that he could get back in Hannah's good graces and then ask to go to Lollapalooza…he really wanted to, but the temptation to instigate a reaction from his mother was too strong.

"So you *are* embarrassed by the fact that you talk to ghosts. So it is not a *gift* after all?" he asks mockingly.

"Mason, it's just the two of us. We need to be supportive of each other, and you are old enough to know that you can't talk to me like that."

"Whatever, Mom." Mason begins to walk away, but Hannah stands up suddenly to say something and accidentally knocks over her glass of wine…it spills all over the couch and the rug.

"Shit!"

Mason looks back at his mom and sees the tipped-over glass and its red contents spewed on the cream-colored furnishings. He knows that he should help clean up, but he is just so angry. He is angry with himself that his plan to ask about Lollapalooza went horribly wrong, but more than that, he is angry that Hannah made everything so difficult for him. Seeing her frantically rush for towels and apply them to the sofa, press down, and repeat just make him annoyed with her. How clumsy.

He is going to walk away, but then he thinks about James, who is waiting for him to ask about Lollapalooza. Mason rushes over and grabs some paper towels from his mom and begins cleaning up the mess.

"I'm sorry, Mom. You're right, I was out of line. I'll clean this up for you." Mason goes to the kitchen and grabs the stain remover from under the sink and begins to spray the stains. He soaks more paper towels on the stain until it is hardly visible.

"Mom, James and I are planning on going to Chicago for Lollapalooza this summer. It's just for two days to listen to some bands and hang out."

"Actually, James's dad and I were talking about it, and we both want to go. I'm thinking the four of us all go together."

"Like chaperones? That's not exactly what I had in mind, Mom."

"Well, I want to see Florence and the Machine…and I haven't been to Chicago in years. The park is enormous. We aren't going to be at the same spot. You'll have your time with you friends, and I'll have mine, and I'll still get the pleasure of seeing you for breakfast."

"No way, absolutely not. That's bullshit!"

"Mason! Watch your mouth or you're not going at all."

Mason rushes toward Hannah and pushes her down. She falls back onto the couch, and while she looks at Mason in shock, he says, "I'm going. And I'm not going with you to watch you flirt with James's dad."

"Mason, that's none of your business. My personal life is my business, and as far as going by yourself, you can't get on a plane without my permission at your age."

"Then I'll take a train." And turning to walk away, he spots a penholder on the table full of pens, pencils, and Sharpie markers. Mason pulls them out into his hand and whips one pen at Hannah's legs.

"Mason!" Hannah shouts angrily.

There is no turning back now. Mason starts throwing the pens, pencils, and Sharpies in quick succession at Hannah.

"How dare you! Stop it!"

When all the pens were gone, Hannah says, "Why do you have to be so difficult? You can't push me, be disrespectful to me, throw things at me, and then be rewarded for it with a trip to a music festival. You know what? Forget it. You are not going."

"We'll see about that," Mason mumbles as he storms out of the room.

CHAPTER 4

LOLLA

Rejection is a challenge.
—Veronica Purcell

The autumn disappears into an icy winter, which melts to a cool spring, followed by a sudden and hot summer. Tickets for Lollapalooza are now available for purchase online.

Mason searches through photos of Lollapalooza from years past. He sees a photo of a group of teens that look like him jumping up and rocking out to some band. They had glow sticks and looked sweaty and completely immersed in the experience. Scrolling back to the top of the page, Mason reads the description of Lollapalooza describing it as an annual summer music festival in Chicago's Grant Park. It hosts over 160,000 people over three days. The bands that play at Lollapalooza range from alternative rock, heavy metal, punk rock, hip-hop, and electronic music.

Opening the top drawer of his nightstand, Mason takes out the pad of paper where he had jotted down the username and password to a small bank account his grandfather had opened for him. There wasn't much in it, but enough "To get you by for a few months in case of an emergency" as his grandfather had put it. It is their secret. Now looking at the website for Lollapalooza, Mason clicks the link to purchase tickets for all three days and then proceeds to buy train tickets to Chicago.

Walking past Hannah's room, Mason sees Hannah folding a pair of shorts into her open luggage. "Mason, wait. I'm sorry you have to miss it this year. But we need to establish some boundaries. Hopefully, next year we can reconsider." Mason gives her a disappointed look in the hopes of stirring feelings of guilt.

A horn sounds outside, and Mason looks out the window. It is Anthony and James. James knows that Mason planned to go secretly to Lollapalooza, but Mason had him swear not to say anything. James told Mason that his dad booked two hotel rooms at the Hilton and Towers, one for James and one for him and Hannah. This is the first time that Mason knows without a doubt that Hannah and Anthony would be together throughout the night. Mason finds it difficult to look at his mother in the face. As if it isn't bad enough that everyone at his school knows Hannah works as a medium, now he has to deal with the anxiety he feels when he is with his only friend, knowing that his mother is sleeping with James' father.

As soon as Hannah is in Anthony's car and he drives away, Mason pulls his backpack that he had packed for Chicago from under his bed and headed out the door. Mason planned with James that the two of them would coordinate via text where to meet so that Mason would not bump into Hannah or Anthony. At night, they would arrange to sneak Mason into James's hotel room.

When Mason arrives by the entrance to the Hilton, he leans against the wall and texts James that he is there. Waiting outside, Mason watches people entering the hotel. Most of them are dressed rather formal. He realizes that this is a rather fancy hotel and is curious to get a better look inside. He walks toward the front door when his phone buzzed. It is a text from James. "Wait! They are coming down now!" But it is too late. As soon as he looks up, Mason sees Hannah's face right in front of him, staring in disbelief.

Anthony stands beside her and shakes his head from side to side.

"Shit" is all Mason can say.

"What on earth? How did you get here? What are you doing here?"

"I just got here. Look, you won't even see me around."

"Mason! You know that's not the point. How could you disobey me like this?"

Then Anthony intervenes. "Hannah, he's here now. How about we just try and enjoy the next few days together?" He pulls Hannah aside and says, "Look, this might be a good opportunity to bond with him. He needs to get used to the idea that we're a couple."

"Come on, Mason, I planned on going to the Billy Goat Tavern on lower Michigan Avenue for a bit of Chicago baseball history. I think you'll like it. Your grandfather was a Chicago Cubs fan, right? The story of the curse of the Cubs started there."

They walk down the cranky metallic staircase from the glamorous upper Michigan Avenue to the grungy lower Michigan Avenue. Entering the Billy Goat Tavern, Mason looks at the walls covered with photographs of Hillary Clinton, George Bush, Bill Murray, and many other celebrities and politicians. They descend the stairs down to the small counter with old tables and chairs on either side, a bar lining the wall to the right, and a chef behind the center counter shouting "Cheeborger Cheeborger!" Mason feels like he is entering another dimension into the diner of a secret society. He feels completely disconnected from the Magnificent Mile above, where droves of stylish people briskly walk on the bright sidewalk adjacent soaring buildings and past high-end shops.

Mason, James, Hannah, and Anthony enjoy their burgers and the Billy Goat Tavern's own craft beer. Then Anthony relays the story. "As the story goes, in 1945, the Chicago Cubs entered game four of the World Series. The owner of the Billy Goat Tavern bought two tickets to that game. That guy, with the goatee, over there," he says as he pointed to one of the many photographs on the wall. "Hoping to bring his team good luck, he took his pet goat, Murphy, with him to the game. At the entrance to the park, the ushers stopped Billy Goat from entering, saying that no animals are allowed in the park. Billy Goat complained to the owner of the Cubs, P. K. Wrigley. Wrigley replied, 'Let Billy in, but not the goat.' According to legend, the goat and Billy were upset, so then Billy threw up his arms and exclaimed, 'The Cubs ain't gonna win no more. The Cubs will never win a World Series so long as the goat is not allowed in Wrigley Field.' The Cubs were officially cursed. The curse lasted until 2016 when the Cubs finally won the World Series."

"Pretty interesting story, Tony. Maybe my mom can reach Billy Goat himself from beyond the grave, and we can hear the story firsthand," Mason says. He and James can't help but snicker at Mason's teasing.

"I can't believe you'd go there again, Mason. After everything that's happened. You're lucky I don't send you back home. I just can't do this anymore," Hannah gets up and goes to the ladies' room.

Mason looks at Anthony and James and says, "Stop staring at me."

"Mason, your mom loves you. What you said really hurt her feelings."

"Of course, you'd know, right Anthony?"

"Mason, you're not making any sense."

Mason gets up, walks out, and James quickly follows behind him. While the day has been stifling hot, the evening cools to warm embracing air. They start to walk along the open pedestrian waterfront in downtown Chicago, passing restaurants, kiosks for boat rentals, and park seating. Mason looks up at the skyscrapers lining the backdrop of storefronts and patrons sitting outside.

At some point, the two young men sit down in an area of wide stairs with several other people to look through their iPhones for tomorrow's lineup of bands. Mason hears chatter and laughter, and when he looks up, he sees the most incredibly attractive girl he has ever seen in real life. She is a few years older than the boys, around twenty-one or twenty-two. She walks to the left of two other girls, who look and dress similar to her but didn't stand out as much. Her hair was a long, blond bob, and her crystal blue eyes are framed by straight bangs. Her very short shorts and cropped top were covered by a sheer fringed shall in line with the uniform style he'd noticed here for girls her age. She smiles at Mason in a way that hinted she has the answers to all the world's mysteries, or at least the mystery that is Mason. Mason feels a tightening in his chest, and his breathing speeds up.

The other two girls have hair that is darker shades of blond but blond nonetheless, like mini mes. They dress similarly in short shorts, cropped tops, and a sheer shawl or kimono-type cover. All three girls are about the same height. Mason thinks to himself how strange it is that young women and girls often make friends with other girls who look similar to them. Or do the similarities come after they are friends?

"Hey, do you have a light?" The prettiest one looks directly into Mason's eyes, but he just stares at her, stumped by the physical reaction she has on him. His heart is beating fast, and he worries that if he spoke, his voice would come out shaking.

Noticing that Mason has become statuesque, James jumps in. "Sure." He reaches into his pocket.

"I'm Helen." She pulls a skinny rolled cigarette from the waistline of her shorts. "This is Laura and Kathryn."

"James."

Unfrozen, Mason introduces himself as well. "I'm Mason." He stands up and asks Helen "Do you have a couple of extra smokes?" even though he and James don't normally smoke cigarettes.

"Sure, here," Helen says as she turns toward Laura with her hand out for the cigarettes. Laura gives them to Helen who hands Mason and James two cigarettes.

"Do you guys live around here?" Laura asks.

"No, we're from Portland, Maine. We're in town for Lollapalooza," Mason replies.

Excited, Helen exclaims, "Us too! Well, I mean, we're going to Lala too, but we live here."

Helen keeps her eyes on Mason almost the entire time, and he is enjoying the way she makes him feel so alive and excited.

She is prettier than her two friends, and the blue-and-white floral shawl with its white fringe complements her striking blue eyes and pale blond hair.

Mason, James, Helen, Laura, and Kathryn talk for a while on the stairs and then get up to walk along the river again. At some point, Helen slides her hand into Mason's. Mason finds the gesture sweet but a little fast for someone he just met. However, there is a part of him that really needs to feel that this girl wants him. He squeezes her hand and slowly lets his guard down. He smiles at Helen, and she smiles back as if he is the greatest man who ever lived. Against his better judgment, Mason lets himself buy into Helen's gaze. For the first time, Mason meets a girl he wants to get to know better. He starts to really like her, and the two exchange phone numbers before their group agreed to call it a night and meet again tomorrow at Lollapalooza.

Before leaving, Helen whispers in Mason's ear, "You're really hot."

Mason smiles and pulls her close to him.

James interrupts with "Get a room, guys," and Helen quickly gives Mason a kiss on the cheek before saying "Good night."

That night, Mason lies in bed and thinks about Helen. It is refreshing to have someone to look forward to seeing the next day. The image of Helen helps him push aside any thoughts of his mom with Anthony. In fact, he begins to feel a little indifferent toward the whole Hannah and Anthony relationship. He is genuinely looking forward to seeing Helen again and building his own first romantic relationship.

The next day, Mason, James, Hannah, and Anthony head down to Millennium Park. Mason likes the gardens and architectural masterpieces like the Bean. Reading from her tourist's guide, Hannah states, "The Bean is a stainless-steel figure that looks like a giant bean. In actuality, the artist who designed it, Anish Kapoor, named it the Cloud Gate. When Chicagoans first saw it unveiled in 2004, they said it looked like a bean, and the name stuck. People love to stand under the curve of the Bean and take pictures of their distorted reflections. Cleaners come twice a day to clean the bottom six feet of the Bean."

Mason and James take a selfie of their reflections under the Bean where they put their arms around each other and stick out their tongues in an ode to Gene Simmons from the band Kiss. Hannah and Anthony take a selfie in a relaxed embrace. Mason is trying to get used to seeing Hannah and Anthony being so openly affectionate with each other, but it is difficult for him to watch, cringeworthy in fact.

They walk to the Art Institute, and Mason marvels at the paintings in the Modern Wing. There are familiar pieces like Grant Wood's *American Gothic*, with the husband and wife farmers standing before their farmhouse with a pitchfork, looking forlorn.

"James, remember my version of *American Gothic* from my art class in junior high?"

James laughs. "The farmer you painted looked like a zombie, and his wife was like a creature from the black lagoon."

Mason laughs too. "Has anyone actually seen *The Creature from the Black Lagoon?* Oh wait, just you, James, just you."

Then there are paintings that Mason has never seen before. Anthony points out paintings by Ivan Albright. Hannah and James agree that the painting is disturbing, but Mason finds the artist's work intriguing. Mason stands before Ivan Albright's painting *And Man Created God in His Own Image,* depicting a somewhat gruesome looking middle-aged man. The style of the painting resembles melting wax or crumpled paper.

After lunch, they make their way through the crowds to Lollapalooza. When they reach the entrance gates, the crowd is overwhelming. It is incredibly hot, and thousands of people line up to get inside. They move in slowly with the crowd of hipsters, and Mason can't wait to part ways with Hannah and Anthony.

Anthony secures private VIP seating at the stadium where Bruno Mars and Jack White would play later that evening. "Anthony, thank you so much for arranging this. I'm not sure I'd enjoy being in that crowd," Hannah says as they look out at the muddy crowd that is gathering by the stage.

It has rained on and off most of the day, and the dirt floor has turned into a sticky and slippery mudslide. Most of the crowd has either taken off their shoes (because they keep getting stuck in the mud) or keep them on if they are laced up tight, the soles now thick with mud. The younger crowd at Lollapalooza is definitely more indifferent to the muddy mess than the older folks who sit on plastic bags on the hill to the side of the stage. At centerstage, a few teen girls are jumping on the backs of their teen boyfriends who gladly give them piggyback rides. Small groups of other kids are playfully falling over onto their friends and into a heap on the muddy floor.

Mason and James sit with Hannah and Anthony but then decide to take a walk to the stage where The Kongos were going to play. "There will be a ton of hot girls there," James says.

"Especially Helen," Mason replies.

The guys arrive at the stage, and Mason immediately scans the audience looking for Helen. They walk all the way to the front of the stage and found Helen, Kathryn, and Laura dancing to a band that Mason doesn't recognize. Obviously intoxicated, Helen dances, twirls, and laughs with her friends while holding a bottle of wine. Mason and James look at each other and know exactly what the other was thinking: "Sucks that they are so strict here about the drinking age." When Helen sees Mason, she smiles and runs over to him, jumping up and throwing her arms and legs around him. He stumbles back but thankfully doesn't fall. Mason is incredibly relieved to see her and realizes that when he is with her, he isn't concerned about anything or anyone else.

The music roars on, and all the kids are dancing. Mason and James jump in and join them. The mud splashes up, and

Helen's legs are covered in it. She kneels down and touches the wet mud with her fingers and then smears lines above either one of Mason's cheeks to look like a soldier in camouflage.

"Now you look dangerous," she laughs.

Mason leans in and kisses her. He is completely submersed in the carefree experience created by the loud music, the dirty, wet mud everywhere, sweaty dancing in the incredible heat, and Helen. The music roars on, but soon Mason notices the lead singer's eyes are constantly on Helen. Mason glances over at her, and Helen is looking right at the singer on stage and smiles shyly at him.

When the show is over, an older gentleman with a "STAFF" wristband and T-shirt comes over to Helen and told her that the band is inviting her and her girlfriends backstage. Mason and James start walking with them but were told "Sorry, guys, just the girls."

"Do you think that's a good idea?" James asks the girls. "You don't know these guys."

"Don't worry, we'll be back soon," Helen says as she walks backstage.

James looks at Mason and says, "Shit, there go our dates."

As Helen disappears behind the stage, Mason sees Wesley. Their eyes meet. Wesley tips his hat and smiles at Mason but then quickly turns to follow Helen and the girls backstage.

Feeling his chest tighten with the sting of rejection, Mason turns to James and says, "Let's get something to drink." He doesn't want to let on how upset he is by the obvious implications of Helen agreeing to meet a band backstage. But Mason knows that James can always sense when he is hurt, and as if on cue, James says, "Look, man, I doubt anything will happen. The girls probably just think it's cool to meet a band that's playing at Lollapalooza. They'll be texting us in a few minutes to meet up again."

The minutes go by, and soon it has been a full hour since Helen, Laura, and Kathryn went backstage. Then another hour passed. Mason and James are going from stage to stage, dancing and talking with all different groups of people partying. Mason is trying to have a good time but is distracted by Helen's leaving and couldn't shake off the negative emotions lurking inside him. He isn't sure yet if Helen rejected him or if she is coming back. That thought makes Mason angry that he could have been so easily misled.

At one stage, a DJ plays electronic music, and the large crowd holds glow sticks and dances in sweaty groups. Mason and James hang out there and dance for almost an hour. People are jumping up and down, and Mason and James join in. Soon they are dripping in sweat.

When they are tired of the fast-paced music and moving lights coming from the stage playing electronic music, they walk onto another stage where all the hipsters hold up their cell phone flashlights the way previous generations held up cigarette lighters. Chvrches is playing "The Mother We Share." They stand there, taking it all in. Later on, Mason and James go to where Imagine Dragons were set to play. When they begin to play their song "Whatever It Takes," Mason feel that it is his own personal anthem. The powerful lyrics light a fire in his chest, and he feels invincible.

All of Mason's favorite bands are set to play over the next few days: The Weekend, Jack White, Arctic Monkeys, and The Kongos, to name a few. They allow themselves to become completely immersed in the experience. Everywhere they look, hipsters sway carefree, and some of the older crowd is obviously intoxicated. A few poor souls sit on the side of the curb vomiting. Mason tries calling Helen a few times, but she doesn't answer.

Mason and James walk along the path to where the food booths are. "No way. Isn't that the place we went to the other night?" James asks.

"Yeah, the Billy Goat Tavern. I guess they have a booth here. Let's grab a burger."

When they finally reach the front of the long line, Mason walks up to the counter and sees a guy in his early forties with dark, curly hair and a Billy Goat Tavern cap at the register.

One employee next to the man says, "We need more cheese slices, Judge."

Mason asks, "Did he just call you judge?"

"Yes, I'm a circuit court judge. This is my family business, so I work here when I can. What can I get you?"

"That's pretty cool. We'll each get double cheeseburgers," Mason orders.

"Two double cheeseburgers!" The judge calls out.

Maybe it is a longing to have a strong father figure in his life right now, but Mason looks at this stranger and says, "So, Judge, I met this girl here, and she acted like she was really into me. But she left to meet a band backstage and now won't return my calls." Although Mason speaks to the judge in a joking manner to hide his despair from James, he aches for someone to give him fatherly advice.

The judge looks at him and says, "Sometimes these things are a blessing in disguise. It doesn't sound like this is a girl worth the heartache if she just took off like that."

"Wise words, Judge," James adds as he nudges Mason to move to the side so the next people in line can order.

Mason's brain tells him that the judge's advice is true, but his heart wouldn't let him feel that Helen's leaving is a blessing yet. His mind keeps reliving how she made him feel while dancing in the mud. How could he possibly be completely irrelevant to her? Losing himself in his thoughts while walking through the crowd, Mason spots Wesley and follows him. He doesn't realize that he lost James in the process.

"Where's Helen?" he asks the ghost.

"She is busy having a romantic and quite intimate time with a very talented musician."

How could that be true? They had an honest connection… is it merely a game to her? Is he only someone she chooses to seduce until someone better came along?

"Fitting that her name is Helen, isn't it?" Wesley goes on as he stops to scrape the mud off the bottom of his shoes against the curb.

"Helen of Troy in Greek mythology was the most beautiful woman in the world. She had a face that launched a thousand ships and began the ten years war." Wesley laughs mockingly. "This is how it is, kid," Wesley says. "If you want these ladies to fall at your feet, you need fame and fortune. Otherwise, git used to being an afterthought like most of these dopes." Mason listens intently. Wesley leans in close to Mason and says, "Let me show you the way."

Mason, in a haze of sweat and heartache, listens as Wesley explains his plan for Mason to enroll in film school and make movies. He walks along the streets of Lollapalooza with Wesley beside him, offering him cigars as he speaks of the glory and fame to come to Mason if he did as Wesley advised. Mason begins to believe that Wesley has the answers to his troubles.

Mason and Wesley turn a dark corner and see Helen leaning in to kiss the lead singer who was on the stage earlier. Mason rushes toward her and without saying a word, pulls her to him.

"Back off!" she yells at him.

"Do you know this guy?" the singer asks.

"I met him last night, and apparently he got the wrong idea," Helen says as she turns away from Mason.

The singer looks at him as if Mason is the biggest loser on the planet. Mason is about to walk away, but in an instant, flashes of him and Helen dancing came into his mind and the taunting way she looked at him. He sees his mom yelling at him at the Billy Goat, remembers how horrible he acted that night he pushed his own mother, and he sees Trent at school smirking at him.

Suddenly, Mason turns around and throws a fiery punch at the singer, narrowly missing Helen.

"Oh my god!" Helen shouts as the singer's bodyguards rush at Mason and pull his arms behind his back.

The singer stumbles up and rubs his jaw. "Let this loser go. He isn't worth the hassle," and he takes Helen by the hand and walks away. His bodyguards let go of Mason and follow their boss.

Fury burns a hole inside Mason. "That's never going to happen to me again," Mason tells Wesley as the sting of rejection and embarrassment begin to transform into determination to prove himself worthy. He would do whatever it takes to be the man everyone wants to be with.

Wesley puts his arm around Mason and whispers, "It won't. Not if you do as aah say. You will go to film school, and aah will help you direct a movie that will make you famous."

Just then, James walks up to them. Only now it isn't them, it is just Mason. The ghost disappears.

"Mason, where did you go, man? Where's your phone? I've been trying to call you." Seeing that Mason is distracted, James grabs his arm. "Come on, walk it off."

Mason begins to tell James that they should go to film school together. "It's the only way for guys like us to be famous and make a name for ourselves. We could do it, James, and then every girl will be following us around. We will be kings."

"Okay, Mason. Um, sure, we'll be famous…like kings."

Over the next two days at Lollapalooza, Mason and James don't see Helen, Kathryn, or Laura, but Mason couldn't stop thinking about becoming a famous movie director.

"Can you imagine being a famous director? We would get to work with the hottest actresses and be on a movie set all day. No one would dare turn us down," Mason exclaims.

James doesn't seem to be as excited about being a movie director. Mason knows that James doesn't quite understand his strong desire for acceptance but is thankful that his only friend goes along with him.

"We could get with Natalie Portman," James says.

"And Jennifer Lawrence," Mason adds.

Monday morning, Mason, James, Hannah, and Anthony pack their bags and check out of the hotel. They still have a couple of hours until their flight. Mason gets a call on his cell phone from Hannah. She tells him that she is sitting in the hotel lobby while Anthony and James walk the Magnificent Mile to buy James a new watch. She tells Mason to come down and join her.

All night, Mason kept thinking about Wesley and his relation to him. Although he doesn't feel like being lectured by Hannah again, he figures he might be able to avoid it by asking her about their family. That way, he can find out more about Wesley as well.

As soon as Mason sees Hannah, he feels disgusted knowing that she had just spent the night with his best friend's father.

Seeing the stern expression on his face, Hannah asks, "What's wrong?"

After a few seconds of silence, Mason replies, "I want to know about our family. About my great-great-grandparents." Seeing Hannah looking surprised, Mason adds, "Grandpa had told me about someone who was a movie director in the family, but at the time, I didn't pay much attention. Now, I wish I had, but Grandpa's gone."

"Not the conversation I was expecting to have this morning, but, um, let me see what I remember…and where to start. Wait. Mason, where is all of this coming from? Is this about going away to college?"

"Maybe. But I still want to know… I am just curious, I guess."

"Okay, well. Let's start with your great-great-grandmother, Charlotte. She died shortly after my grandmother, Clara, was born. Grandma told you the story years ago. Do you remember?" she asks.

"Vaguely. It was a long time ago," Mason says.

Hannah goes on. "It was a terrible accident at a speakeasy in Boston. Apparently, the roof was weakened by a fire and collapsed on the people dancing inside, including Charlotte.

Charlotte's husband, Wesley, left Boston and came to Peaks Island to raise Clara in a quiet, nurturing place away from the noise and media attention in Boston. I'm sure Grandma told you that Wesley was a movie producer and director. Charlotte was an actress, also his muse. They became quite famous although there was always some negative publicity surrounding Wesley. That's the part I doubt Grandpa or Grandma told you. He had a bad reputation for being overly aggressive with several female actresses and had taken advantage of at least one of them. Every family has its secrets."

"Except for the Villas family," Mason says.

"I'm sure they have some old secrets in their family line somewhere too, Mason."

"Tell me more about Wesley. He sounds pretty interesting."

"Well, my grandmother always spoke very fondly of her father. She said he was very charming, and even though he moved to the East Coast from South Carolina in his twenties, he continued to dress like the Southern gentleman of his youth throughout his life. Although I do remember my grandmother saying that he wasn't home with her that often. He spent days at a time in Boston or New York on film sets, and she was often cared for by a nanny. It wasn't until Clara was an adult that she learned her father had been accused of any misdeeds against women. He spent many years fighting those allegations but eventually died of a heart attack before his name was cleared of any wrongdoing. Unfortunately, Wesley spent a large amount of his fortune from the film industry prior to his death. What remained of his legacy is our house on Peaks Island and a small trust fund."

Mason thinks about Wesley. Even if he has done something to those women, no one knows the whole story. *Maybe they were leading him on, and he was tired of their games,* Mason tells himself. He thinks about Helen and feels camaraderie toward Wesley.

Hannah continues with their family history. "As you know, my mom met my father while she was studying at Boston University but never married. They were very much in love but did not believe in formal marriage, an idea that was blasphemy at the time. What they really wanted was a child. It took them many years before they finally conceived. Remember how both of them never seemed to rush anywhere? They were always like that. I think it was because they had to wait so long for a baby, and Grandma would always say how during that time nothing else mattered more or was worth hurrying about. My mother and father went even further in their liberal beliefs by giving me my mother's last name, Hunter, rather than my father's name. Remember how often they talked to you about their days as professors at Boston University? They loved the campus and working close together."

A memory of his grandfather comes to Mason. His grandfather was sitting in the four seasons room of their home in

Peaks Island and looking out at the ocean. Mason had just finished breakfast and went in to say bye.

"What are your plans for the day, Grandpa?"

"I'm going to sit right here and enjoy my tea while watching the waves. I thought I'd be bored in retirement, but you know what? I love it. I love not having a plan for the day. I might go for a walk later. Or read a book. Maybe I'll invite a friend over. I've got everything I need. Seeing you, your mom, and your grandma happy is the most fulfilling part of my life. All the other stuff in life is peanuts compared to you guys."

Hannah smiles at her own memory of her father and says, "I miss them so much. I miss Dad's calm, gray eyes and my mother's quick wit. Your grandparents loved you very much, Mason. When I met your dad, Aiden Peters, similar to how my parents met, in college, I thought it was meant to be. I kinda wish we were staying here an extra day so I could show you around Loyola University where Aiden and I studied biology. At the time, I wasn't sure what I wanted to major in but was always very good at science, especially the study of life. Aiden was fun to be around and always came by my apartment to pull me away from my studies and go walking along the beach of Loyola's beautiful Lake Shore Campus."

Mason interrupts his mom. "Mom, you just said you weren't sure what you were majoring in when you were in college. Why are you putting such pressure on me to get into business administration or something boring like that when you didn't even know what you wanted? And, anyway, it's not like college served you any good. Are you working as a biologist now? Not really. More like a dead-ologist."

"Mason, you do not get to judge me. I am your mother. You haven't been where I have. Why would you ruin a perfectly nice conversation, the first one we've had in a very long time, by making rude comments like that? I just don't get you, Mason."

Mason shrugs, knowing his mom would rather not continue arguing. Sure enough, regaining her composure, Hannah continues. "When Aiden and I became pregnant with you during our senior year, Aiden had already planned to move out to California after graduation to study marine biology on the West Coast. I knew he wasn't ready to be a dad and distanced himself from me as much as he could those last few weeks of school. By the time you were born, Aiden was already living in California. He wasn't a bad guy, Mason. I've told you before how he was smart and ambitious, he just wasn't ready for fatherhood. He had no intention of moving to Peaks Island, whereas there was no place I'd rather be. I had enough money in my trust fund that I didn't care that Aiden wasn't around. Plus, your grandparents were thrilled to have their grandson close to them."

Every time Hannah speaks about Mason's father, Mason feels pain and hurt. He hates that he can't control feeling that way, but it is a wound that wouldn't heal. He often wonders why his father never cared enough to meet him after all these years.

"Mom, I've been thinking about it, and I really want to study to become a film director."

"A movie director? Seriously, Mason? Are you just trying to hurt me? Honey, please. Don't start thinking like that. Is it because of Wesley? Wesley lived a long time ago, and things were different then. You can't base your future on the career of a dead ancestor. You need to focus on something more practical. Plus, you have that scholarship to BU!" Hannah begins to raise her voice. "Mason, you have to stop this nonsense and focus on getting a real degree!"

"I'm not just going to be some loser with a boring business degree! What the hell am I going to do with a business degree? Manage your séance business? Right this way, ghostly freak, payment is due in full at the front desk!"

Just then, Anthony and James appear through the doors and begin walking toward the table. "Check it out," James says, extending his left arm out. "It's a Tag Heuer Carrera, you won't believe the features this watch has. And it just looks freakin' awesome."

CHAPTER 5

JAMES

Some people aren't loyal to you. They are loyal to their needs of you. Once their needs change, so does their loyalty.

—Author unknown

After Lollapalooza, the remaining few weeks of summer went by quickly. Fall came and went, as did winter, and then spring. Mason completed his senior year of high school in an uneventful blur of classes, weekend parties, exams, hockey, and more classes, weekend parties, exams, and hockey. Against Hannah's wishes, he enrolled at the New York Film Academy.

Even though the previous summer at Lollapalooza Mason and James had agreed to attend film school together, James reconsidered when he returned home to Maine. He told Mason he changed his mind after thinking about his future more clearly. Instead of film school, James was admitted into

New York University where he planned on studying Business Management and Environmental Science in the hope of continuing and growing his father's grocery business.

Both in New York, Mason found part-time work giving tours at the MET, and James waited tables at a farm-to-table restaurant to pay for the rent they shared and personal expenses. They were busy with their studies and part-time jobs but manage to get out on the ice a couple times a week to play hockey together.

Being roommates as opposed to friends who see each a few hours and then retire to their respective residences, Mason finds it difficult to hide his secret from James. He knows James begins to notice odd things about him. Like how he would sometimes look at the wall as if someone is there, when no one is. At breakfast one morning, Mason looks up from his bowl of cereal and nods in agreement to Wesley telling him that his future is bright and is on his way to achieving the fame he always wanted. Then he sees that James is staring at him, confused, since Mason is acknowledging someone invisible to him. Mason just smiles to James but could sense that it has the opposite effect and just makes him look creepier. Is he losing his best friend?

At night, Mason is talking to Wesley in his bedroom and says, "No one has what you do. I want that. I want it all."

Then he hears a knock on the door and the sound of James turning the knob. Of course, being the polite guy that he is, James pauses before opening the door a crack. "Mason?"

After a second of silence, Mason replies, "Hey, what's up?"

"I thought I heard talking in here. Is someone else here?"

"Huh? Oh. No, no one else is here. Just giving myself a motivational speech…it's my daily mantra."

Mason knows that James was too smart to believe him but also too nonconfrontational to delve deeper into the issue. So an awkward silence lingered for a moment before James just says, "Oh, yeah, that makes sense. I knew I heard talking. Take it easy, man. See you in the morning."

The next night, Mason wants to ensure that things are back to normal between them. He walks the few blocks to the restaurant where James works, knowing his shift is over in ten minutes. He looks inside the restaurant and sees James wiping down the empty tables. He suddenly feels unsure about his decision to just show up at James's work. Maybe he is being too obvious and trying too hard to act normal? He decides to send James a text message instead: "Meet me at the hockey rink in about thirty minutes?"

"Boss is making me stay late tonight. Place is packed."

Shit. James is on to him. He can't lose his best friend. He would have to try something else.

But the next afternoon when Mason arrives to their apartment, he finds James sitting on the couch reading notes from a lecture on the future of business management.

"Hey, you want to go grab a slice of pizza?"

"Um, actually, I was just about to head out to the campus library…for, a, um, study group."

Mason watches James nervously pack up his backpack. Is his childhood friend afraid of him?

After James left, Mason goes to his room and puts on his grandfather's watch.

"What a simple timepiece," Wesley says with a bullying smirk as he watches Mason wrap the strap around his wrist. "You can tell a lot about a man from his timepiece. And this one," Wesley says as he takes Mason's arm and taps on the glass, "says a few things, but success is definitely not one of them."

Mason looks at the worn black leather strap and plain silver circle around the face of the watch, and for the first time, Mason can't feel endearment for his grandfather. He takes off the watch and shoves it into his drawer. Suddenly, Mason hears the front door open.

"I forgot my phone," James says as he reaches across the counter and grabs his phone just as it begins to ring. "Hey, Dad," James says.

Mason waves a hand as if to signal he would give James some privacy to talk to his dad. But as soon as he turns the corner, Mason leans against the hallway wall to hear what James and Anthony are talking about. Would they talk about him? Would James tell Anthony that Mason is weird or odd?

"I've got some great ideas for environmentally friendly waste management and food production for Tony's. Dad, we could totally incorporate a lot of it in our prepared meals section."

Okay, maybe Mason and James's friendship is intact. Maybe James isn't going to talk about him behind his back. But something else irks him now. What is it?

James's relationship with his father is a source of tribulation for him. Mason doesn't want James to know that he is jealous that his own father isn't around. But the way James spoke to Anthony just now on the phone...isn't he bragging? Is he trying to make Mason jealous because he no longer sees Mason as a friend?

When he hears the door close again and Mason is certain James left, Mason bangs his fist against the wall until it bleeds. Was James ever really his friend if he could turn on him like that? Is sympathy the foundation on which their friendship is built?

"He won't pity me when I'm a famous movie director. He'll be begging to be my friend, they all will."

CHAPTER 6

THE CHASE

Jealousy, the dragon which slays love under the pretense of keeping it alive.

—Havelock Ellis

On the first day of directing 101 class, Mason puts on his dark-gray jeans and black V-neck shirt. Wesley appears briefly to offer vague advice and words of encouragement: "You will need to step outside the box, my boy" or "grab hold of that slippery fish."

Mason combs the long strands on the top of his hair back and clasps on his brown leather and silver wristband that Hannah had bought for him right before he left home for school. He is lying to himself if he thinks he doesn't miss her. For so many years, it has been Mason and Hannah, Hannah and Mason. Her words often coming into his mind even when he isn't expecting it, "If you hang on to the past, you won't have any room for the new experiences that are waiting to come into your life. That's how people get stuck. Don't let yourself get stuck, Mason."

Mason grabs his bag and walks out of the building. After a few blocks of walking on this perfect seventy-three-degree, sunny September day, Mason enters the dark subway train and grabs a seat. At the next stop, Mason looks up just as the doors open. He feels his heart quicken as a young woman with the most perfect dark-chocolate-colored skin Mason has ever seen walks onto the train. Her hair is flipped over to one side and fell into a voluminous cascade of tight dark curls several inches past her shoulder. Her black upturned eyes are shaded with a glistening light gold shadow and perfectly framed by black lashes. Her high cheekbones sit prominently between a straight, strong nose. With her full lips tinted red and cream-colored off-the-shoulder top revealing sun-kissed shoulders, she is beautifully exotic. Her long, orange skirt is linen with buttons from the waist down to her midcalves, the last two buttons intentionally left undone. She glances in Mason's direction. She gives him a slight smile before finding a seat across from him. Then she looks directly at him and he at her.

"Hey." Her lips moved slowly as she begins to speak, and Mason fights a natural inclination to move in close toward her. He wants to catch her scent, touch her smooth skin. But then he remembers Helen and how her pretty face and smile fooled him into thinking she was genuinely interested and felt a wall build up inside him. However, he likes that this girl looks different from Helen. Aside from this girl's much darker complexion, her posture is very upright, and her lean physique is muscular, indicating years of self-discipline in some kind of sport, unlike Helen's waif, thin body.

"Hi." Mason smiles, and from the way she looks at him, he thinks that maybe she feels an immediate attraction as well. "That's a really beautiful necklace," Mason says.

"Thank you. I bought it at little boutique near my place," she says as she touches the rectangular bronze tag that hangs vertically from its chain around her neck. The tag has a cross carved out of the center.

"Skylar Jackson," she says as she extends an arm. Unlike Helen, her gestures are mature, and the manner in which she speaks is more friendly or professional than flirty.

"Nice to meet you, Skylar, I'm Mason. Mason Hunter." He reaches for her hand and tries to linger in its grasp for a second, but Skylar politely smiles and pulls her hand away. Mason finds comfort in sensing that Skylar is somewhat guarded, like he is, and that maybe her intentions are not to play a childish game like Helen did.

"I'm getting off at Rector Street," Skylar says.

"So am I," Mason replies, pleasantly surprised.

At the same time, they say, "The New York Film Academy."

After that day on the subway, Mason and Skylar are inseparable. They spend endless weekends at the MET. Skylar would linger around Mason as he gives tours, and on their free time, they sit in the indoor garden in the Asian wing. Or they roam through Greek and Roman art. They walk through the Iron Wall in the Medieval Art section to the Robert Lehman Collection and stand in awe of masterful works of art.

In the Temple of Dendur in the Seckler Wing, Skylar pretends to be an Egyptian goddess commanding Mason. "You will obey me, servant, or face the consequences," she whispers in his ear as she slowly turns to face him.

Mason is in awe of this creative and outspoken young woman. She is incredibly fun to be around. Her comments always make Mason laugh, and she knows more about art and culture than anyone Mason has ever met. In film school, Skylar surpasses all their classmates.

But it wasn't her success in film school that draws Mason to Skylar. It was her confidence that somehow miraculously lacks the arrogance that usually accompanies it. Mason thinks that Skylar seemed remarkably comfortable at all times and didn't compare herself or show any envy toward anyone else. There is an ease with which she walks and talks that says, "There is no place I'd rather be on this earth than right here, right now, at this moment."

Mason realizes he is in love with her. Skylar is his muse, his inspiration. He feels love for her, but that love is bound to the intrigue and danger he feels when he is with her. As Wesley would appear with his musings that Skylar would leave him,

Mason feels a sadistic kind of love for Skylar. Although he hasn't verbalized it to himself yet, he loves the torture he feels in his heart being pulled in different directions: the path of pure love he sees in Skylar's eyes and the dangerous demise of his soul if he ever does lose her. The thought of returning to a life before Skylar seems unbearably dull. Skylar is Mason's key to an exciting life. The key to a bright, shining future creating movies with the woman he loves, far away from the judgmental eyes and hateful looks of his neighbors at Peaks Island. Or if she leaves him, the crushing defeat to his entire being, and what that would make him capable of is too exciting to walk away from.

Standing in the Temple of Dendur, surrounded by gray stones and a dark-gray pool behind them, Mason looks at Skylar, and the people around them seem to grow quiet. He leans in toward her until his lips meet hers in their first kiss. As they slowly pull away, Mason is overjoyed to see Skylar's eyes smiling with love as well.

Unfortunately, Mason's loving feeling only lasted a second. Over Skylar's shoulder, standing fifteen feet way, Mason spots Wesley. Wesley is looking at the museum exhibits but suddenly turns and looks directly at Mason. Then Wesley moves quickly without his feet touching the ground until he is only an inch behind Skylar. Wesley's eyes are red and angry. "Enough of this, Mason! I didn't lead you to film school to fall in love. You are here to find fame and take what is yours! A woman's love will destroy you!"

Mason wants to believe that Skylar wouldn't break him as Wesley warned, but his life of being an outcast and his experience with Helen's trickery created a fear of rejection, and a cold indifference creeps in. He tries to shake it off and return to the feeling of light in his heart, but he couldn't regain that moment, it is gone.

Looking at the bleak expression in his face, Skylar's smile melts. "What's wrong?" she asks.

"Nothing. I'm fine," Mason replies as he fakes a small smile. He knows he doesn't want to lose her, but what if Wesley is right and Skylar would only break his heart? Mason tells himself that he has to keep his guard up, just in case Wesley is right.

Mason and Skylar continue walking through the museum and admiring different works of art. Skylar always expresses her awe of portraits of beautiful women who lived over one hundred years ago. Mason sees how captivated Skylar looks as she stands before *Portrait of Madame X* by John Singer Sargent.

Pointing out the painting to Mason, Skylar says, "Look at the contrast of her white skin against her sexy black dress. It's uncanny that the dress is the type of dress a woman in the year 2018 might wear, not what one normally envisions on a lady in the year 1883, right?"

Mason nods in agreement as he looks at the painting even though he doesn't understand much of anything about women's fashion. The dress is a markedly deep black with a plunging neckline and jeweled straps.

"Who was this woman and what was her life like? If a picture speaks a thousand words, a painting can speak a million. Without a doubt, the woman in the portrait shared a deep intimacy with the artist. Only a special connection like the kind between lovers could create such a telling stance," Skylar says as she looks at the woman posing in the painting. She adds, "Madame X is looking away in her portrait, suggesting she is hiding something, yet her body language speaks volumes of subtle sexuality."

Mason looks closer at the painting and mischievously asks, "You got all that from a painting of a woman in a black dress?"

Skylar draws down her chin and looks up at Mason, shaking her head left to right in a teasingly disapproving manner. "Tsk, tsk."

When Skylar sees Paul Gauguin's painting *Two Tahitian Women*, she contemplates it as well. "Two seemingly simple, naive, young women, one holding mango blossoms, in the midst of what appears to be a casual everyday activity for them. Yet here they are, hanging in the Metropolitan Museum of Art in New York, over one hundred years later, for all to admire."

Mason adds, "You left out the part of both of them being topless." Skylar laughs, and they continue on.

Mason and Skylar pass paintings by Claude Monet. When they saw Claude Monet's *Jean Monet on His Hobby Horse*, Mason says, "Look at that little boy wearing a dress. In elementary school, I did a report on President Franklin D. Roosevelt and came across a picture of him as a child dressed like a little girl. It was so bizarre, but I guess in 1884 when the picture was taken, his white skirt and shoulder length hair were considered gender neutral. Little boys wore dresses until the 1920s. Actually, all babies wore only white until the midnineteenth century when pink and blue became options for babies, but it wasn't until decades later that blue was designated for boys and pink for girls."

"That's it. Someday I'm going to have a boy and dress him in pink, and I'll dress the girl in blue," Skylar says smiling.

Mason laughs and replies, "Poor kids."

On comfortable weather days, when one would need only a light jacket or warm sweater to be outdoors, they spend long days in Central Park. They sit in canoes and take turns paddling. Usually Mason paddles, but occasionally Skylar would take over and Mason would teasingly shake the little canoe. They could walk around the park for hours. Whenever possible, they would wait until the sun begins to set and the black streetlamps that lined the path are lit. Still light enough to see the ponds and greenery yet dark enough for their path to be illuminated. That is Mason's favorite time of the day.

Every few weeks, they would splurge on tickets to see the Frick collection at the Henry Clay Frick House in the Upper East Side in Manhattan. There, Mason would pretend he is Henry Frick, and Skylar would play the part of his wife, Adelaide Howard Childs.

Loudly clearing his throat, Mason would begin, "Yes, I am Henry Frick, and it gives me great emotional satisfaction to fill my library, living hall, Fragonard room, and dining room with priceless works of art. Here, I can roam through my mansion, room by room, and admire each of my collection pieces."

"Oh, Henry, enjoy our beautiful home. At least you will be acknowledged generations from now when they turn our home into a museum. I, on the other hand, will be mentioned here only as an afterthought. As tourists sit in the music room and watch a video of our lives, our move from Pittsburg to New York because of the dangers to our family during the steel strikes, and every piece of furniture and work of art collected, will be attributed entirely to you. As if I, who is your wife and partner, lived in a box, unable to provide any input. Truly, history has been devastatingly forgetful of every woman's input in their family's triumphs. Alas, all the credit will be yours, dear Henry."

Mason wraps his arms around Skylar, pulling her close to him and then tickles her sides. Skylar laughs as she pulls away. Holding hands, they continue to wander around the Frick House until they completed the audio tour of each painting and how the Fricks acquired it.

Giovanni Belini's masterpiece, St. Francis in the Desert, is Skylar's favorite. Mason knows she would always stop before this painting and stare at it transfixed. The painting depicts St. Francis as he receives the stigmata, the wounds of Christ's crucifixion. The image of St. Francis freely giving himself over to God is expressed in the way only a masterful artist can portray and left Skylar with a feeling of falling to her knees.

When they first see the paining, Skylar tells Mason it makes her recall an incident a few months prior. "I caught the influenza virus and was overcome with a dangerously high fever. Lying in bed, I began to hallucinate. It was so weird, but I saw myself kneeling on my bed with my hands in a prayer position as a ray of light came into the room. I heard a voice, 'Are you ready to leave this world behind and join me?' Don't laugh. I know it's weird."

"I'm not laughing…go on."

"Well, I felt a strong love and conviction unlike any I ever felt and replied to the voice, 'I love you and only you my Lord. I am your humble servant, now and forever. Please, take me from this world and let me be with you.' Then I fell asleep. But the memory of the intense feeling of love during that experience and the ease with which I willingly agreed to give my life to God stayed with me. It haunts me somewhat, having felt a surrender of myself to God and death that I did not think I was capable of, I don't even regularly attended church or pray. Can you relate to any of this?"

"Sorry but no." Mason tries to hide a smile, and Skylar nudges him, "Thanks for making me feel like a freak."

Mason finds Skylar's willingness to share such private moments foreign. He couldn't bring himself to share anything about Hannah, her séances, or Wesley with anyone. But for the first time, he feels that maybe he could talk to Skylar about those things. *Not today though,* he thinks to himself.

Central Park and the museums are the epitome of what Mason loves about New York. When he would walk out of Frick House or the MET, Mason feels as if anything was possible. After seeing the masterful art created by humans over hundreds and thousands of years, Mason gains a stronger sense that he cannot leave this world without creating his own masterpiece. Each visit leaves him more determined to create something more in this world worth admiring, as humans have done throughout history.

Times Square, on the other hand, is a madness of crowds, invading smells, and dizzying lights that Mason avoids at all costs. All the inspiration and peace he feels in Central Park or after an afternoon viewing art would undergo a grotesque metamorphosis into frustration and agitation after only a few minutes in Times Square. Mason would occasionally catch a glimpse of Wesley turning a corner or tipping his hat to Mason before disappearing in the crowd. He has seen Wesley every few weeks appear somewhere in a crowd or leaning against a building before quickly turning a corner and disappearing again.

One day, as Mason stands outside Skylar's building waiting for her to come down, Wesley suddenly appears beside Mason. It is spring, and people are emerging outdoors with every opportunity to enjoy the first warm sun after a long cold winter. Skylar lives on the top floor of a three-apartment building located in the neighborhood of Soho, New York. The cobblestone street across from Skylar's place is lined with art galleries, shops, and cafes. Mason looks around the neighborhood and thinks to himself that it seems as if it is made for Skylar. She belongs in Soho, with her artistic soul and ease of spirit. As Mason would learn later, Skylar's parents own the tan, brick, three apartments as an investment property and rented out the lower two floors.

"Hey, kid. I see cupid shot his arrow into your heart again with this one, eh? All I can do is warn you again, Mason," Wesley says as he puffs his cigar. The anger he has shown that day in the museum is gone. Wesley seems to have resumed his Southern gentlemanly manner.

"What are you doing here? Why do you keep lurking around here? Leave before she comes down," Mason whispers as he tightened the grip on the collar of his dark-gray plaid shirt, pulling it closer around his neck and hoping none of the passersby heard him. He is angry and annoyed that Wesley had ruined his first kiss with Skylar and keeps appearing to antagonize him. But at the same time, Mason realizes just then that he isn't sure he wants the ghost to leave for good. He is overwhelmed with his love for Skylar, the pressure of film school, making it to work on time, and paying his rent every month. Mason always has an itching fear that he could mess up and lose it all. He knows that he could easily be replaced at work with the museum, and if that happens, he wouldn't be able to pay his rent. His school projects keep him up late at night, and more than once he had shown up late to work and faced an angry boss. Some of his classmates' ideas and work are so incredible that Mason questions his own ability. He aches for someone's guidance and reassurance. He wants someone to tell him that it will all be okay. Since Wesley is the only one to keep showing up and offer advice, skewed as it may be, Mason begins to believe him.

Agitated, the spirit takes on a serious tone. "Listen to me carefully. Do not forget that I was the one who guided you to this film school. I am the one who sent that idea into your skull. We have work to do, and you falling for this girl was not part of the plan. She has a different purpose to serve, and it isn't to keep you warm at nights. I made sure she got on that train when you did so that you would meet, but I did not think you would fall in love with a black girl. We need her only for her idea."

Mason couldn't quite make sense of what Wesley is saying. He knows that Wesley's warning about Skylar is breaking his heart, but what did Wesley have to do with Mason and Skylar meeting?

"What are you talking about? How could you have had anything to do with how Skylar and I met? What idea of hers are you talking about?"

Wesley explains how he caused a passenger to trip and fall on the train platform on the day Mason and Skylar met. This caused several people to miss their train, and Skylar ended up on the same train as Mason. Wesley tells Mason that he had been watching Skylar for a long time and knows that she has a brilliant idea for a movie. Wesley's plan was for Mason to get to know Skylar, build trust with her, and when she confided in him what her idea is, Mason would take it from her.

"I know it's in her head, but I can't see what it is. You see, some of us ghosts can see when someone has a profound emotion or brilliant idea. When someone is feeling that emotion or thinking about a new idea, their aura changes into a vast array of gold and indigo. I saw Skylar with a glorious rainbow of indigo as she jogged past me one day. I knew something was happening inside her, but I could not see what it was. So I followed her into her home and saw her pouring over books on directing movies, studying old and new methods for script writing, etc. I knew then where she was headed. Take her idea and make it your movie, Mason. It will be your first big hit and propel you to stardom. After that, there is no limit to what you can do."

"This is crazy. Anyway, even if what you say is true, why would Skylar just let anyone, even me, take this idea of hers?"

"She won't let you," Wesley goes on. "You have to take it from her and then finish her."

"Finish her? Wait. Just wait. Oh my god. Get out of here. Get out of here now! There is no way in hell that I would ever do what you're implying!"

"Calm down, Mason. You don't get it yet. You can make women do whatever you want once you're famous. Don't fall in love with them, Mason. They will only let you down. They will only fall in love with someone else in front of you and crush your soul. I've been around a long time and have seen it time and time again. You must take from her what you need and keep going."

While Mason has secretly longed for Wesley to reappear every once in a while, he doesn't know what to make of Wesley's ill-fated and murderous advice. Before he can say another word, Wesley is gone.

A little shaken, Mason tries to regain a calm appearance as Skylar steps outside, looking as beautiful as always as the wind blows her hair away from her face. She wears a lace shawl over a pale pink tank and ripped blue jeans. Her lips are painted a dark gothic red. Mason knows he can never hurt her.

Mason has promised Skylar that they would go to Lindy's Deli for cheesecake. Skylar says that Lindy's had the best cheese-cake in the world, and she has gone way too long without a slice. As the two of them walk through that crowded Times Square on their way to Lindy's, Mason sees an artist on the side-walk spray-painting his work before a crowd of onlookers. They stop, and when the artist looks up at Skylar, he stops his work and just stares at her. When Skylar looks directly at this street artist and their eyes meet, Mason sees a connection between them that makes him very uncomfortable.

Just then, everything and everyone around him stop. The oversized movie screens and every single person in Times Square come to a silent standstill. Mason looks at Skylar and realizes that her eye contact with the artist is frozen in time as well. He studies Skylar and tries to read her thoughts from the look in her eyes as she gazes upon this stranger. The only thing Mason can decipher for certain is that he doesn't like Skylar looking at another man. He feels the green bile of envy and doesn't know how to fight that feeling. It isn't a welcomed sensation, and Mason needs someone to tell him that he cannot control every person in his life. That he needs to enjoy his time with Skylar, whether it be for a short time or for the rest of his life. But Mason isn't fortunate enough to be given that kind of advice. He never could get the words out to explain to Hannah or anyone how he is feeling and how confusing life, and the afterlife with its visiting ghosts, are.

Instead, Mason has Wesley. Mason sees him walk through the motionless crowd and the song "Feel It Still" by Portugal. The Man began to play. Wesley starts dancing like Fred Astaire tap dancing to "Puttin' on the Ritz." With his hat and a walking cane, Wesley tap dances to the beat of "Feel It Still" and sings along to the lyrics. "Remember what I told you, Mason. It's already happening…she will leave you for someone else."

The jealousy Mason feels only grew greater, and he wants to scream and run away with Skylar. And just as strange as the whole dance scene begins, Wesley disappears back into the crowd, and everyone around him returns to the present time.

Looking again at Skylar and the street artist, Mason tries hiding the rage he feels from Wesley's words that created a lump in his throat. He says "Hey" to break their focus on each other. "How long does it take you to finish one of those?"

"It depends. This one is almost done, and I started it about an hour ago. But I lose track of time a lot when I'm working on them," the artist explains as he picks up a different color can of paint and continues spraying. He then looks back up at Skylar and asks, "Do you like it?"

"Yeah, it's really beautiful. You are very talented. I'm Skylar, by the way. This is Mason."

"Hi, I'm Chase." Chase wears a black skullcap and a yellow sweatshirt, the kind you might pick up at a Walgreens or CVS that reads "I Love NY." His hazel eyes reveal a calm focus. His face is covered with at least three days of stubble, which Mason usually considers to reveal a man who lacks good personal hygiene, but Chase's perfectly straight white teeth indicate that he is unshaven as part of his style, which annoyed Mason.

"Chase? Isn't that a character from the kids' Disney movie *Cars*?" Mason asks as he chuckles.

"I don't think so, but I'm not much into kids' movies these days so can't say for sure. What did you say your name was, Maltese?"

"Funny. It's Mason. Keep up the good work. We gotta get going," Mason says as he takes Skylar's hand and gently pulls her away.

After less than a minute, they hear a voice, "Wait up!" Mason and Skylar turn around and see Chase in a light jog coming up behind them. Pulling the cap off his head revealing light brown messy hair, he says, "I just finished my last painting and thought I'd join you guys if you don't mind."

"Sure," Skylar says before Mason has a chance to speak. "Have you had Lindy's cheesecake? It's the best."

"I can't wait," Chase says as he smiles at Skylar and gives Mason a wink.

Mason, Skylar, and Chase squeeze into a booth at Lindy's. It isn't long before they are enjoying their dessert and laughing like old friends. Chase definitely has a way about him that is endearing. Mason can see that Chase was someone who easily makes friends. He is charming, and Mason thinks he sees attraction and intrigue in Skylar's eyes when she looks at Chase. Wesley's words reverberate in Mason's head, making him paranoid that Skylar is falling in love with this guy. His jealousy makes it seem that Skylar hangs onto Chase's words like a child to a master storyteller.

Wesley's words come back to Mason, "They will only fall in love with someone else in front of you and crush your soul." He does not want to believe it. Helen comes back into his mind for the first time since he met Skylar. But what he and Skylar have is special, could she so easily fall for someone else? Could it happen so soon after Wesley gave that crazy warning? Those thoughts and questions make Mason want to lash out. He imagines himself pulling Skylar from the booth and dragging her out of the deli as everyone stares at them in disgust and fear. Instead, he swallows his anger and allows a cold numbness to spread inside him.

"So are you from New York?" Skylar asks.

"Yes, pretty much all of my family is from here. My last name is Zacharias, and if you meet anyone else with that last name, chances are that he or she is from New York and either an aspiring actor, artist, or writer. We all somehow followed a creative path. My grandfather told my cousins and me that our ancestors were from Romania and traveled in a circus. Probably gypsies. But no one knows for sure, and my mom said he made that up. Personally, I believe it. It makes sense to me considering not a single person in my family works a regular nine-to-five job."

Skylar tells Chase about the chance meeting on the train with Mason and how they are both headed to film school. Chase goes on and on about how he loves movies and says that his favorite movie was *The Aviator* starring Leonardo Di Caprio. Mason agrees that it was a good movie but not his favorite. Mason prefers works by Quentin Tarantino. He loves *Pulp Fiction, Inglorious Bastards,* and *Django Unchained.* Skylar accuses Mason of overlooking *Kill Bill* because the main characters were mostly female.

"*Kill Bill* was a huge success and used female main characters in the martial arts scenes. Mason, if the same exact movie had all male characters, you would have it in your top five," she says.

"Who said it isn't in my top five? It's just that if I am going the martial arts route, I'd probably go *Crouching Tiger Hidden Dragon* over *Kill Bill*, but if you want real kung fu movies, you have to go back to Bruce Lee movies. Bruce Lee films are the real deal," Mason replies.

"I loved *Legends of the Fall*. One of the best movies ever, by far," Skylar states.

"I have to agree that it is a pretty awesome movie," Chase says.

Just the fact that the two of them are agreeing on movies makes Mason more and more uncomfortable. He finds himself squirming in his seat as his attempt to hide his jealousy became more and more difficult. Finally, Mason decides that he needs to break up this threesome for the night.

"Well, Skylar and I should probably start heading back. I'm sure we'll catch you around. We'll look for you painting in Times Square the next time we want a third wheel on our date."

Chase chuckles. "Don't be so easily threatened, Mason. I just thought you guys were cool and wanted some company. My two best friends went to the West Coast for college this year, and I found myself with no one to hang out with these days."

"Don't be a jerk, Mason," Skylar adds. "Here, Chase." She takes Chase's phone and says, "Unlock it." Chase puts his thumbprint on the phone, and it unlocks. "I'm putting in both mine and Mason's numbers in here. Next time you want company, call us," she says.

As they head back to Skylar's apartment, Skylar says, "That wasn't right, Mason. I hadn't seen you as a jealous guy before, but you were so possessive just now. I don't want you to act like that again."

"Seriously, Skylar? What I don't like is someone butting in on a date. Who does that? Would you go up to a couple you just met and invite yourself to join them? That's weird. Something is up with that guy."

"It's not weird, Mason. I wish people were friendlier. Everyone gets stuck in their own little iPhone world. It was refreshing to have someone just want to meet people face-to-face right off the bat."

"All right, Skylar. I'm not going to say I agree, but I would *sort of* be able to see your point if you hadn't just given your number to a guy right in front of me." Mason chuckles, but his underlying emotion is still visible by the hurt in his eyes.

"It wasn't like that! Don't twist the situation into something else. There's nothing wrong with being friendly. I gave him your number too, Mason. What do you think I'm going to do? Sneak off with Chase behind your back? I mean, really, Mason, you can't think that little of me."

"No, of course not, Skylar. You *obviously* wouldn't sneak off. You'd do it right in front of my face." Mason has been trying to sound somewhat playful during the argument, but the more they talk about it, the more frustrated and angrier he becomes.

They both stand there silent for a few seconds. Mason looks at Skylar, and she is intently looking back at him. He couldn't hold eye contact and looks past her.

"Come on, let's go," Mason says as he grabs her hand.

As Skylar and Mason approach Skylar's place, Mason is relieved that she hasn't let go of his hand and hopes she isn't angry with him anymore. The sun is shining so bright in Skylar's place. Mason watches his beautiful girlfriend open the fridge and pull out a pitcher of Sangria.

"I made this for us. Let's sit out on the balcony and have a glass or two or three," Skylar says as she examines her glasses for any smudges.

Mason is intrigued that Skylar can let go of their argument so easily. But Mason keeps hearing all the doubts that Wesley placed in his mind. He doesn't want to lose Skylar, and he suddenly grabs her wrist almost instinctively. He slowly moves his hand up her arm to her shoulder. Fingering the collar of her dress, he makes his way to the front center where the buttons sit. One by one he unbuttons them and lifts her slightly off the ground as he buries his head in her neck. His kisses are forceful and passionate. He lifts her, and Skylar wraps her legs around his waist.

In the bedroom, Skylar slides down his body and onto the white comforter on her bed. Her sheets are crisp with a light floral pattern. The sheer white curtains blow gently from the open window, letting in a breeze that is just a little too cold.

"Hold on," Skylar says as she gets up and turns on her UE Roll speaker. On her phone, she presses the Pandora App, and from the speaker, "Connected By Love" by Jack White starts to play.

Afterward, they lay side by side. Skylar props herself up. "Mason, I have this idea. An idea for a movie."

Mason remembers what Wesley has said about Skylar having an idea, and he feels his blood freeze.

"I want to remake *Gone with the Wind,*" she says.

Mason is somewhat relieved. This is the brilliant idea that Wesley was talking about? Maybe Wesley is wrong, about everything. First of all, everyone knows that a classic like that should never be remade. It could never be as good as the original. Regardless of that, a remake is *already* in the works starring Reese Witherspoon and Matthew McConaughey. Or is it made already? Mason isn't sure, but either way he knows it isn't or wouldn't be a success.

Skylar goes on. "I know what you're thinking. Bad idea. But I wouldn't dare remake *Gone with the Wind* word for word, scene for scene, like the original. I'm thinking about a remake of the story set in modern times."

"What do you mean?"

"Well, it's a classic. But have you read it, Mason? As beautiful as the prose in the story is, the book is riddled with racism.

While the female characters are shown to be incredibly strong, especially for a book written in the 1800s, black people, *my* people, are described as unintelligent, weak, and it's just so… degrading. I have to change it. I will rewrite it. The story will take place in modern times, and I will have strong black actors play lead roles so that *Gone with the Wind* will have a new meaning in this country forever."

"Wow, Skylar. That's a huge undertaking. I think it's a great idea. Let me know how I can help."

Mason feels a chilling unease not because he had any intention of stealing Skylar's idea and harming her as the ghost suggested but because he feels himself being pulled in a direction that maybe isn't of his choosing after all. If Wesley has designed for Mason and Skylar to meet and for her to confide her idea to him, how much of what happens next would actually be within Mason's control?

CHAPTER 7

LIGHTING A BONFIRE

Anger is one letter short of danger.
—Eleanor Roosevelt

For the first Thanksgiving since Mason and Skylar met, Mason invites Skylar to Peaks Island with him and James so she could meet Hannah. Anthony would be there too. Mason pictures Anthony sitting close to his mom, maybe an arm around her, making himself at home in Mason's house, and his stomach turns at the thought.

Autumn is Mason's favorite time of year. His mother fills the front yard with garden croton, chrysanthemums, pansies, and of course, mums. The garden and trees are afire in oranges, yellows, and reds. The picturesque island with its American

Flags, beautiful fall gardens, and crashing waves make the most perfect Thanksgiving backdrop.

Coming up the walk with Skylar and James, Mason sees the look of excitement on Hannah's face. She quickly opens the door with a smile. "Mason! I missed you so much!" she says, embracing her son in a tight squeeze. "And, Skylar, I am so excited to meet you!"

The two women hugged as well, and then Skylar says "I'm very happy to be here" as she hands Hannah a container. "Oatmeal cranberry cookies. Mason and I baked them together."

Hannah looks at Mason with a pleasantly shocked expression. "Wow, what a healthy relationship."

During occasional phone conversations, Mason tells his mom about Skylar and how smart and pretty she is. He also tells her that the two of them are spending a lot of time together. Now here they are, ready to celebrate Thanksgiving. Hannah grabs Mason again and squeezes him. "You definitely leaned out a bit over the last year."

Mason takes in a deep breath. "The house smells amazing. Rosemary, thyme, and everything nice."

Mason has mixed emotions about being home. He misses Hannah and is initially happy to see her, but as he walks into the family room, he feels the presence of a recently departed ghost. He knows that Hannah must have had a séance the last few days, and Mason is quickly reminded of the ridicule he endured growing up on Peaks Island because of his mom's meetings with ghosts. Sometimes, he is tempted to shout at Anthony the revelation that Hannah is a crazy lady who speaks to dead people. Then again, Anthony might just think that Mason is the crazy one, so he keeps quiet and lets Anthony go on believing that Hannah is more of a social worker and that the ghost stuff is just rumors.

All his thoughts about Wesley, Skylar, Anthony, and Hannah leaves Mason oblivious to the fact that while traveling to Peaks Island with James and Hannah, James has been watching Mason carefully for any signs of the peculiar behavior he often witnessed in their apartment. At one point, while Skylar is asleep on the bus, James sees Mason smiling and nodding at someone. Then he turns and looks at an attractive girl in the row across the aisle from him. He smiles at her very flirtatiously and proceeds to move his eyes up and down the girl's long legs. James finds it unnerving and creepy, considering Mason's seeming love for Skylar. It doesn't make sense. What James can't see is that Wesley is beside Mason. Wesley points out any and all attractive girls along their way and made comments to Mason like "This is what you're missing by sticking with one girl. Life is too short not to taste a little of everything."

In the kitchen, Anthony and Hannah work around each other naturally as they put the finishing touches on Thanksgiving dinner. Mason sees the two of them together and remembers the many Thanksgivings that he was the one helping Hannah with the holiday meal. Seeing Anthony taking his place makes a lump rise in Mason's throat. Although he is an adult in his twenties, he still feels that his future was uncertain and longs to have his mother unequivocally on his side. But now as he watches Hannah and Anthony reach over each other to grab a spice bottle, Mason feels his lifelong cheerleader slipping farther away from him. Pained, Mason decides to join James and Skylar sitting in the family room. James and Skylar are making casual conversation about turkey stuffing but quieted when Mason walks into the room.

"They've moved in together," James tells Mason.

"They look really happy," Skylar interjects.

Mason just shrugs and takes another sip of his cabernet sauvignon. Holding up his glass, Mason says "Cheers" and takes another sip.

"Should I offer to help in there?" Skylar asks the two young men.

"Do you really want to?" James snickers.

"Just relax with us. They're fine," Mason says.

"All ready!" Hannah shouts.

The group move to the dining room. Hannah has set the table the night before with her Lenox plate settings in gold and white. Waterford Thanksgiving patterned linens covered the table, and Baccarat crystal stemware is perfectly placed. Crystal candlesticks are lit with white candles, and Hannah has strewn decorative fall leaves throughout the table. The Lucullan feast includes a golden brown turkey with oranges and lemons sliced in half around its platter. Smooth red cranberry sauce, mashed potatoes, oven-roasted sweet potatoes, green beans with mint, and a lush salad of mixed greens, glazed and roasted butternut squash, and a pomegranate dressing and marinade create an incredible color of flavors to indulge in.

At the head of the table, Hannah stands and begins to say a prayer. "Let us offer thanks for our food and the blessings around us. Let us be a source of hope for those in need. Let the feelings of love, kindness, and a well-directed yet gentle spirit always be reflected in our actions."

"That was beautiful, Hannah," Anthony says. He walks over to the head of the table, kisses Hannah quickly on the lips, and begins to carve the turkey.

Mason cringes, seeing the affection between Hannah and Anthony. What if Anthony finds out that Hannah and Mason could, in fact, see ghosts? Now that Anthony and Hannah live together, Mason wonders how long it would take Anthony to realize that Hannah speaks to people who aren't there. (It hasn't crossed Mason's mind that his roommate is realizing odd things him.) The outcome of such a revelation can be devastating. Mason fears that Anthony would confirm the rumors that the Hunters are crazy. The thought of Anthony breaking Hannah's heart is infuriating. Sitting on the side of the table next to Skylar, Mason looks on in discomfort as someone other than himself or his mother is carving the Thanksgiving turkey. He feels displaced in his own home.

In high school, all the other kids thought James's dad was "pretty awesome," as they put it. Anthony was a self-made success who worked really hard and also happened to look really cool. He was fit and dressed in a style similar to his son, jeans and button shirts rolled at the sleeves to just below the elbows. Anthony would pull up to their school in his Jeep, having just returned from a three-day weekend in London with James, looking like Sean Connery and Daniel Craig in some new father-and-son version of *James Bond*.

Mason notices that both Anthony and James have matching Tag Heuer watches. He wonders what it would have been like growing up as Anthony's son, having a father who is always there.

After dinner, Hannah brews a pot of coffee and puts out the apple pie for desert. She scoops out the vanilla ice cream on each plate and drizzles homemade caramel sauce on top. As they enjoy their dessert and coffee on Hannah's linen sofa, they avoid any talk of politics and instead discuss their schools, work, and plans for Christmas break. Mason and Skylar tell of how they met by pure coincidence on the train and headed to their first day at the Film Academy together.

"When you meet the right person, you just know," Anthony adds. Clearing his throat, he goes on, "Since the first moment I met Hannah, I knew she was someone special. But not just anyone special, she is the only woman for me." From the nervous excitement in Anthony's voice, Mason knows where the conversation is heading. Mason gets up quickly and "accidentally" knocks over his glass of wine.

"Oh no, hold on," Hannah says as she rushes off to get some paper towels. Mason looks up to see James looking at him in disbelief that Mason would try to spoil what Anthony is about to say. But it doesn't work.

Hannah returns and is about to clean the mess, but Anthony stops her. She looks at Mason and says, "We have something very exciting to tell you. We're engaged!" With that, Hannah pulls out a sparkling diamond ring from her pocket and slips it on her finger. The band is simple platinum gold, but the diamond is an impressive five karats. "We wanted to tell both of you in person," Anthony adds as he looks at James.

"Congratulations!" James says.

Then Skylar congratulates the newly engaged couple as well, but Mason gets up and walks out of the room. Skylar follows him.

"I'm going for a walk," Mason says.

"I'll come too," Skylar replies.

"So am I," James adds.

Before going out, Mason grabs a couple of craft beers from the fridge in the garage. Mason, Skylar, and James walk down the street just as Trent Stellar drives by. He looks right at Mason but looks away, smirking. Just a reminder to Mason of the teasing he endured on the island.

"So, Skylar, do you like hockey?" James asks, trying to ease the tension.

"I like watching sports, but I was never much of an athlete," Skylar replies.

"But she's very flexible," Mason adds. Skylar nudges him, and they all laugh a bit at Mason's comment.

"Up here there's a spot where James and I would hang out a lot," Mason says as they turn down a dirt road. Past several trees, the path leads to a flat, rocky cliff's edge that overlooks the ocean. The ocean waters are a grayish blue as the autumn sun is setting behind a cloud-covered sky. The waves crash onto the rocks below, splashing white foam into the air before rolling it back into the sea.

"Wow, it's beautiful," Skylar replies.

It is getting colder outside, and James suggests a small bonfire. They trace their steps back near the trees and gather some logs, dry twigs, and tinder. James and Mason show Skylar how to arrange the logs and sticks perpendicular to each other and then place some logs upright into a tipi formation. James reaches his arm into the tipi and lights the tinder inside with his lighter. As the flicker turns into a flame, Mason looks over at Skylar and smiles at her.

He wonders if his girlfriend is enjoying her first visit to Peaks Island. Mason really wants to show her how beautiful it can be, especially after his negative reaction to the news of Hannah and Anthony's engagement. But as much as he doesn't want to screw things up with Skylar, Mason's thoughts keeps returning to the awkwardness of Hannah and Anthony living together. He is struggling to be present and in the moment as his mind keeps wondering off.

Mason, Skylar, and James warm their outstretched hands over the fire as they sit a few feet away from it on logs. Mason puts his arm around Skylar. James looks at both of them and then gently pokes Mason's leg with a stick he is holding in his hand and says, "Mason and I would bring our hockey pucks up here and practice our slap shots. There must be thousands of hockey pucks at the bottom of the ocean right here," he points out into the darker gray water. The sun has almost set, but the fire is keeping away the chill in the air.

"Wait, you would shoot pucks into the ocean? What if some poor sea creature tries to eat it and chokes?" Skylar asks, concerned.

"We didn't think about it at the time. Never crossed our minds, actually," James explains as he and Mason both snicker.

James inserts the stick into the bonfire and sparks flow as the blaze grows. "Now, I can't imagine throwing anything into that water. This past year I took a class on environmental pollution, and it was kind of shocking. There is so much pollution in the ocean that the water is incredibly acidic. There is so much plastic in there that it's tragic, really. Just think about how much plastic we use in a single day and how different that is from just a few generations ago. We go out to eat, and we use plastic cups, forks, spoons, and straws. We go grocery shopping, and everything gets put into plastic bags. Plus, with Amazon and everyone shopping online, everything is packaged into plastic bags and then put into boxes, every day, for millions of people. All this garbage eventually makes its way into streams, rivers, and eventually oceans. None of it is biodegradable. Fish choke on straws, turtles get stuck in those plastic things that keep cans together, and so forth and so on. People used to use only reusable glass and silver to eat, and groceries were packed in paper only. Most people don't even know how to use kitchen towels now. They just rip off another piece of paper from the paper towel roll, which is also packaged in plastic, every time they need to wipe a drop of water from the counter. Then the noise pollution from these huge boats messes up signals and communication for whales. That's why you see those strange pictures pop up of beached whales. They get confused because the waves and noise we create mess up their communication system."

Mason stands up and walked to the edge of the cliff. "Blah, blah, blah," he says. Mason finishes his beer and tosses the bottle into the ocean.

"Mason! I can't believe you just did that!" Skylar shouts angrily.

"Seriously, Mason, you could be such a jerk sometimes," James adds.

With that comment, Mason lunges at James and knocks him over.

"What the hell, man!"

"Just having a little fun," Mason replies.

"The wasn't fun. You can be such a dickhead sometimes," James says.

Mason looks as Skylar and sees her clenching her fists together against her chest. She looks scared.

"Whatever, let's head back," Mason answers. He brought Skylar to the cliff to escape the agitation he feels being around Hannah and Anthony, but now he has to deal with his best friend competing for his girlfriend's admiration. How frustrating. What's worse, Mason knows that Skylar is impressed with James's knowledge and concern for the environment. James is winning.

Skylar puts her arm around Mason. "Mason, it's going to be fine."

CHAPTER 8

LAISSEZ-FAIRE

I loved something I made up, something that's just as dead as Melly is. I made a pretty suit of clothes and fell in love with it. And when Ashley came riding along, so handsome, so different, I put that suit on him and made him wear it whether it fitted him or not. And I wouldn't see what he really was. I kept on loving the pretty clothes—and not him at all.

—Margaret Mitchell, *Gone with the Wind*

Three years later, Mason and Skylar are finally graduating from film school. Skylar pours her heart and soul into writing the script for her version of *Gone with the Wind*. She begins by spending months studying the original book until she feels she knows the characters personally and understands what drives them to do what they did.

Gone with the Wind was written by Margaret Mitchell in 1936. The story is a drama of the Civil War that begins in the spring of 1861. Skylar enjoys how beautifully written the book is from the first page. She loves how the detailed description of the main character, Scarlett O'Hara, who is the most pursued Southern belle in her neighborhood, makes the reader feel that they actually knew her. In the book, Scarlett's mother instills the Southern manners and charm expected of ladies at that time, but the author hints to the reader that there is much more to Scarlett under the surface than polite Southern charm.

Skylar can immediately connect to this young girl who has to show one face to the world while feeling another way beneath the surface. More than once in her life, the world showed her that there is not a clearly defined and acceptable space in society for an outspoken, beautiful, and intelligent black woman. She recalls how during her first week of film school she openly disagrees with a male classmate. What was his name? Jason? Jake? Skylar couldn't even remember his name now, but she remembers his face…but even more so, she remembers the lesson she learned.

Standing before the class, the professor poses the question: "Self-direction and self-control motivation technique is used under…anyone? Yes, you with the yellow top."

Skylar stands up. "Laissez-faire style."

That's when that guy "Jason" says, "Basically, it means not doing anything. A director who doesn't direct." His friends nod in agreement.

"If you have excellent actors, why couldn't you trust in their creative genius to help build on yours? Let them have the freedom to create in collaboration with the framework you've laid out," Skylar replies.

Their professor smiles and says, "Excellent point."

Skylar thought it was an inconsequential discussion, but she was wrong. Calling out a male colleague meant that she would be intentionally left out of every group project for months to come. Furthermore, as the majority of professors in film school were male, it appeared easy for her male classmates to establish camaraderie with their teachers, whereas she became an outsider. From that day on, Skylar learned to tread lightly around the male ego if she wanted to succeed in her career. Fighting them only made it harder to squeeze her way into the inner circle of the directing world.

Skylar continues her study of *Gone with the Wind* and what parallels to modern life she can generate. Scarlett's father is a determined Irish peasant farmer who became wealthy. Her family is upper middle class and owns Tara, a large plantation near Savannah, Georgia. Although an immigrant, his hard work and success allowed his family into the upper echelon of their society. As the story unfolds, the reader learns that young Scarlett is quite a snobbish bully. She dislikes and looks down on just about everyone except the boy she has a crush on, Ashley Wilkes. She spends her time thinking about colorful dresses, flirting with all the boys who like her, and dreaming about marrying Ashley. However, one day, she is devastated to learn that Ashley is engaged to Melanie Hamilton. She cannot fathom how Ashley could prefer someone Scarlett considers as plain and uninteresting as Melanie to herself. She decides that if Ashely knows how Scarlett feels about him, there is no way he could turn her down. The next day, Scarlett is at a barbecue at the Wilkes plantation and confesses to Ashley her desire for him. Ashley tells Scarlett that although he loves her, he is marrying Melanie because she has more in common with him than Scarlett does. Angry, Scarlett slaps Ashley and leaves the room. Just then, Rhett Butler, an outcast for having not married a girl he dated, surprises Scarlett by revealing that he had been listening and watching the conversation between Scarlett and Ashley. He compliments Scarlett on reacting to Ashley the way that she did, but Scarlett is angry with Rhett for eavesdropping.

Reading about the parties and teenage drama in Scarlett's life brought memories back to Skylar. Skylar's father is also a self-made success story who brought up his daughters in an affluent suburb and earned the acceptance of his community by his upstanding reputation in the medical field. But unlike Scarlett, Skylar is never a bully. As the only black family in her neighborhood, Skylar always struggled with acceptance.

The first week of her freshman year of high school, a group of the popular girls approached her and invited her to a party that weekend. They said that one of the girls' older sisters had her driver's license and would pick her up so they could drive to the party together. All that week, the girls invited Skylar to sit with them at lunch, talk about boys and where to shop for clothes, etc. Skylar thought it was great how friendly and accepting they were. That Saturday night, Skylar dressed up and waited for the girls to come pick her up. But no one showed up. After a while, she tried calling them, but no one would answer. She sat in her room and opened up her Facebook page. There, she saw the girls were already at the party and had posted pictures of themselves posing in group photos. Skylar was crushed, and she couldn't help the tears from streaming down her cheeks. When her mother walked into her bedroom, she asked, "Skylar? Aren't you going? What's wrong?"

After Skylar explained what happened, her mother tried to find some explanation that hinged on a misunderstanding.

"No, Ma. They are just wicked, and I feel sorry for them. I pity them that they can be so cruel. I couldn't be so mean, even to get back at them. I pity them 'cause they must have a lot of garbage in their souls to be that mean. Pieces of shit. All of them."

Her mother was stunned. Skylar knew her mother desperately wanted their family to fit in. That day she learned how strong she was and that she could handle these girls.

Monday morning at school, she walked by the bullies and sat down next to a quiet girl she had noticed the week before and introduced herself. She never let the bullies know it hurt, and they gave up on trying to bully her. She vowed to herself to never be a cruel, nasty person like them.

Looking back at that memory, Skylar feels proud of herself and the strong young woman she's always been. She feels a strong obligation to her younger self to succeed in this project of remaking *Gone with the Wind.*

Skylar tries to imagine what modern challenges occurred in the past decade or so that she could use in *The Remake* so that Skylar's version of Scarlett can emerge at the end as an incredibly strong and resourceful pioneer woman, as did Scarlett. Skylar carefully traced Scarlett's journey from spoiled teenager to independent woman.

After the Civil War begins, Scarlett agrees to marry Charles Hamilton, Melanie's boring brother, out of spite and hopes her engagement will hurt Ashley. Sadly, after Scarlett and Charles are married, Charles joins the army and dies of a disease. Then Scarlett learns that she is pregnant with Charles's baby. The baby is a boy whom Scarlett names Wade. Scarlett considers children a nuisance and hardly shows her son any love.

Bored and unhappy, Scarlett decides to take a trip to Atlanta, Georgia, and visits Melanie and Melanie's aunt, Pittypat. She yearns for the days where she wasn't required to wear black mourning clothes and avoid social gatherings. Scarlett becomes happy and busy in Atlanta helping care for soldiers in a nearby hospital and begins to spend a lot of time with Rhett. The relationship between the two characters is an interesting one as Scarlett's Southern values leads her to find Rhett's bluntness and teasing offensive and infuriating. Rhett, however, tries to convince Scarlett to abandon Southern expectations that widows go through a long mourning period and live very conservatively and modestly.

The Civil War rages on. From a young spoiled girl, Scarlett's strong will and determination inherited from her father begins to shine through. She becomes hardened by the war after a shortage of food and clothing in Atlanta. Scarlett and Melanie fear for Ashley, who is fighting in the war. Ashley was at the battle of Gettysburg and is captured by the Yankees. The Yankee army makes its way to Atlanta, and Scarlett wants to return to her plantation, but she has promised Ashley that she would stay with Melanie, who was pregnant with Ashley's baby. Melanie considers Scarlett wonderful, but Scarlett harbors secret spite for Melanie's sweet and quiet demeanor. She despises Melanie even more for being a burden now in the face of her promise to Ashley.

The Yankees capture Atlanta and set fires everywhere there. While the fires are blazing, Scarlett has no choice but to be a midwife to the birth of Melanie's son, Beau. Rhett returns and rescues Scarlett and Melanie by leading them out of Atlanta. Once the ladies are outside the fires of the city, Rhett leaves them to join the Confederate Army. Scarlett braves many dangers all through the night and throughout the next before finally arriving at Tara. Once at Tara, Scarlett learns that her mother, Ellen, passed away. In his grief, Scarlett's father, Gerald, went insane. To make matters worse, Yankee soldiers looted Tara. There was no food or cotton on the plantation. Scarlett becomes a scavenger to survive and promises herself she would never experience such hardship again.

Eventually, Scarlett begins rebuilding Tara. She has to go as far as murdering a Yankee who is trying to steal from her. Another Yankee sets a fire that Scarlett put out. When the war finally ends, many soldiers return home and so does Ashley. One of the soldiers lost a leg and is homeless. His name is Will Benteen, and he stays at Tara and works on the plantation. Will Benteen learns that a government official who used to work at Tara raises the taxes on the plantation. The government official, named Jonas Wilkerson, plans on the O'Haras not being able to pay their high taxes, and Jonas could buy the plantation for himself. In a panic, Scarlett devises a plan to seduce Rhett Butler in the hopes that he will give her the money she needs for the taxes. Although Rhett became immensely wealthy after the war, he is in a Yankee jail unable to access the funds for Scarlett. Then Scarlett decides to visit her sister's boyfriend, Frank Kennedy, in a second attempt to obtain money needed for taxes. Scarlett betrays her sister and marries Frank, who pays the taxes, and Tara is saved. Frank owns a general store, and Scarlett focuses on improving his business.

After Rhett gets out of prison, he lends Scarlett money to buy a sawmill. Scarlett becomes a successful businesswoman, contrary to the expectations of Southern society. After her father dies, Scarlett invites Ashley and Melanie to move to Atlanta and share in Scarlett's lumber business in an attempt to keep Ashley close to her. Then Scarlett and Frank have a daughter, Ella Lorena. One day, two men, one black and one white, attack Scarlett. The Ku Klux Klan avenges the attack on Scarlett, and in the fight, Frank dies.

Scarlett quickly accepts a wedding proposal from Rhett, and they have a long honeymoon in New Orleans. Upon their return to Atlanta, Scarlett builds an enormous and fancy mansion. She keeps company with wealthy Yankees. Scarlett and Rhett have a daughter together, Bonnie Blue Butler, and Rhett adores her. He tries really hard to be accepted back into Atlanta society so that Bonnie isn't negatively affected by her parents' reputation. At first, Scarlett and Rhett have a happy marriage, but soon Rhett grows more and more distant toward Scarlett.

As for Ashley, Scarlett no longer desires him but rather considers Ashley a good friend. However, Ashley's jealous sister spreads a rumor that the two are having an affair. Scarlett is surprised that Melanie defends Scarlett's reputation. Sadly, Bonnie dies in a horse-riding accident, and Rhett is devastated. Rhett and Scarlett's marriage worsens. Soon after, Melanie suffers a miscarriage, and Scarlett rushes to her side. Melanie asks Scarlett to care for Ashley and Beau. Scarlett comes to the realization that she loves her friendship with Melanie and doesn't have romantic feeling for Ashley at all. Melanie has experienced the same hardships as Scarlett during the war and meets them with equal courage and grace.

Scarlett determines her true love is Rhett. Unfortunately, Rhett tells Scarlett that he no longer loves her and leaves. Scarlett is crushed and lonely. She becomes determined to come up with a way to win back Rhett's love.

Skylar begins working on her script and aptly titled it *The Remake*. *The Remake* begins in the spring of 2007. The main character, Amber Daniels, is a wealthy black socialite in Manhattan. Her days are filled with Pilates, yoga, tennis, brunch at fancy hotels, extravagant gatherings with the elite upper middle class, and playing friends with the numerous men who want to date her. Amber's family made their wealth from her grandfather's real estate business. They own a beautiful estate in Long Island. She is infatuated with one of her suitors, Liam Hamlin. Amber always makes an extra effort to look her best when its likely she will encounter Liam during one of their social gatherings. Liam would always flirt with Amber, leading her to believe that he would soon ask her out on a date. However, Liam ends up dating Emma Slavin, who is the daughter of the business partner of Liam. Eventually, Liam and Emma become engaged, and Amber agrees to go home with David Slavin, Emma's brother and someone Amber has little genuine interest in. David is over the moon that Amber chose him, and it's not long before he proposes and she accepts. Amber's promiscuous friend, Rob Lexington, tries telling Amber that she shouldn't rush marriage or marry someone for the wrong reasons, but Amber disregards his advice.

Then, in December 2007, the Great Recession in the United States hit. The United States experienced a severe financial crisis and deep recession. Many of the people in Amber's life either lost their jobs and or their homes. David Slavin loses his high-profile job and moves out of state. Amber stays in Long Island and soon after realizes that she is pregnant with David's baby. Lonely and bored in her parents' Long Island home, she decides to take a trip to Manhattan and stays with David's sister, Emma. While enjoying busy Manhattan, Amber's friendship with Rob evolves into a romantic relationship. However, Rob ends up being accused of securities fraud and is eventually placed on house arrest.

Unfortunately, the recession becomes apparent everywhere. The stock and real estate markets are crushed, destroying $18.9 trillion of household wealth. Many businesses are forced to close, and numerous storefronts are vacant. Amber's family's real estate business is hit hard when the housing bubble bursts, and their Long Island mansion is under foreclosure. Liam becomes obsessed with saving his accounting firm that is close to going out of business. He spends most nights in the office to avoid the loss of time and cost of transportation. Liam asks Amber to stay with Emma, who is due to have Liam's baby any day.

Liam's business goes under, and he cannot afford their Manhattan apartment. Amber and Emma return to Amber's family home in Long Island while Liam stays back in Manhattan and tries to find employment with a former competitor's firm.

Emma gives birth as soon as they arrive in Long Island. Amber's parents packed up and left for Europe. Amber is shocked to find squatters in her family's home. She forces the squatters out and begins cleaning up the house. After several weeks, Liam secured new employment albeit at an enormous salary cut, which was a miracle given that during the recession, eight million people lost their jobs.

Amber finds that she must hustle to save her family's home. She manages to keep her family's real estate business afloat by borrowing money from a former fling, Jeffrey Hayes. Jeffrey has a movie theater business that remained unaffected by the recession. Amber and Jeffrey begin dating and marry quickly thereafter. Amber becomes very involved in Jeffrey's business and finds ways to make it more profitable. Amber invites Liam and Emma to become franchise owners of one of the movie theaters. Sadly, Jeffrey dies in armed robbery one night, leaving a new theater that was just built in a shady part of town.

After Jeffrey dies, Rob is finally cleared of all charges against him and proposes to Amber. Amber accepts, and they build the grandest mansion in Long Island. At first, Amber and Rob share a happy marriage, but it isn't long before Rob misses his promiscuous lifestyle and is unfaithful to Amber. Rob is disgusted with himself, realizing he ends up a cheater. To deal with his disappointment in himself, he begins to resent Amber and blames her for his feelings of being tied down.

As for Liam, Amber no longer desires him but rather considers Liam a good friend. However, Liam's jealous sister spreads a rumor that the two are having an affair. Amber is surprised that Emma defends Amber's reputation. Nonetheless, the accusation worsens the marital issues between Amber and Rob.

Soon after, Emma suffers a miscarriage, and Amber rushes to her side. Emma asks that Amber agree to be the legal guardian to her children should anything ever happen to her and Liam. Amber realizes how deeply she loves and values the close sisterly bond she shares with Emma and that she doesn't have romantic feelings for Liam at all. In fact, Amber determines that her true love is Rob. Unfortunately, Rob tells Amber that he no longer loves her and leaves. Amber is crushed and lonely. She becomes determined to come up with a way to win back Rob's love.

*****

Skylar and Mason plan on directing *The Remake* as a team. The couple manage to keep in touch with Chase as well. He and Mason become friends, and Skylar suggests Chase to be involved with the set design. They are well underway with their film project using funds from various producers who sought out young talent from the New York Film Academy. In particular, Chase's uncle has become a successful producer over the last few years and is eager to help his nephew and his nephew's friends succeed in their project.

While Skylar and Mason direct the film together, they work closely with Chase in explaining the vision for the film. Surrounded by a team of actors, actresses, and producers, the threesome spent any and all their free time talking about *The Remake*.

Making *The Remake* takes place over a year. Before casting could begin, Skylar and Mason meet with lawyers to resolve any potential copyright infringement issues. Then casting begins with the role of Amber. Numerous actresses try out for the part. Mason is immediately drawn to Madison Harper, a twentysomething actress who begins her career as a swimsuit model and recently appeared in small movie roles. Tall with dark-blond hair and grayish-blue eyes, Madison Harper is the type of girl all the other girls wanted to look like when they are growing up. The type that seemed perpetually in excellent shape, with perfect white straight teeth and shiny hair.

"Skylar, she's perfect as Amber."

"I'd have to change the script, Mason. Amber is black. That's crucial to my movie."

"You mean *our* movie, Skylar. We can cast black actors to play Emma or Liam, but Madison is perfect for the lead role. We need someone who looks like that to sell this movie."

"How do you not understand what this movie means to me? I wrote the script with Amber as a black woman in mind the whole time. I can't envision her differently, and it changes the purpose of this whole thing. I want a black woman to play this part."

"We can cast other black actors, Skylar. You are a black female director. You have opened the door for so many black women already by what we are about to accomplish…but first we have to make sure that our first movie is a success. It *has* to sell. People will buy tickets to see Madison as Amber. Give her a shot, please."

Skylar reluctantly agrees to the role of Amber being given to Madison. Soon the role of every character is filled with actors and actresses that Skylar and Mason agree on, and the filming begins. Madison is doing a great job playing Amber. She looks great in the stylish clothes chosen for her and seems to be in her element when filming called for her to pull up in a sporty Mercedes or sip a fancy cocktail at a Long Island club. But when Madison plays the part of Amber flirting with male friends, Skylar notices that when Mason comes up to Madison to direct her to use more body language when flirting in a scene, she would lean into Mason and practice on him rather than one of her costars. Skylar begins to see that Madison is definitely flirting with Mason, but she couldn't tell if Mason is giving Madison any signs that he likes her in that way.

At the end of the day, Skylar approaches Mason. "Mason, Madison is quite a little flirt, isn't she?"

"She plays the part very well."

Agitated, Skylar sarcastically says, "Look, I know that life has changed a lot for both of us in the last year. And if you want to take a break from us and explore what it's like to be a director with women throwing themselves at your feet, now is the time…"

Mason cuts her off, "Wait, what? Skylar, no. I am not interested in random actresses like that. I am crazy about you. I've adored you since the first moment I saw you on the train, and I don't want to take a break from us."

Skylar hugs him, and when she looks up, she sees Madison watching them. When they make eye contact, Madison quickly flashes a smile.

CHAPTER 9

THE WORLD IS HIS

I can resist anything except temptation.
—Oscar Wilde, *Lady Windermere's Fan*

The premier for *The Remake* is a tremendous success. Hundreds of people are in attendance, and after viewing the film, Skylar and Mason receive a standing ovation. The after party was at the Plaza Hotel. The actors all look fabulous, and everyone with their close friends and families are in high spirits celebrating the film. Hannah, Anthony, and James excitedly watch the premiere while seated in the same row as Mason.

Hannah leans over to Mason and says, "Mason, I am so proud of you. I know this movie is going to be a huge success."

Skylar's parents, who helped produce the film, come to celebrate as well. Mr. and Mrs. Jackson are a very attractive and well-dressed couple in the their midsixties. It is clear to Mason that Skylar inherited the best physical attributes from each parent. He compliments Mrs. Jackson on her stylish appearance.

"You look incredible, Mrs. Jackson. I can see where Skylar gets her good taste. How long will you be staying?" Mason asks.

"We are hoping to catch a show tomorrow night and then head out Sunday morning after breakfast," Mrs. Jackson replies.

"I know it's late, but if you and Mr. Jackson are up for it, we'd love for you to join us for a late-night feast at this incredible Greek restaurant called Avra. Best seafood ever, I swear."

"That sounds wonderful, Mason, thank you," Mrs. Jackson replies.

"Then it's set. Skylar and I will meet you there."

Mason wonders if he made a mistake asking Skyler's parents to meet them for a private dinner. What if Skylar thinks he means to take their relationship to the next level? A marriage proposal perhaps? He is surprised to feel that he dreaded the prospect of an engagement. He loves Skylar but doesn't feel ready for marriage.

As they were about to get in their Uber car, Mr. Jackson says that he forgot his medication and that they would have to stop at the hotel first.

"I'll come with and help you get another Uber from your hotel to Avra," Skylar says.

"Okay, I'll head out to Avra and wait for you there," Mason says.

Mason watches as Skylar and her parents drive off. Just then, Madison comes up to Mason.

"Mason, I just want to thank you for this opportunity. The movie turned out so well. You are going to become a famous director!" Madison says as she squeezes his arm.

"You were great, Madison. I think you are the one who is going to become famous."

Then Madison leans in and kisses him. "Wait, Madison…"

But Madison cuts him off before he can finish, "Just come with me, Mason. I want to do something for you. Something special to show you how much I really appreciate the opportunity you have given me. Casting me as Amber was the best thing that could have happened to me."

Mason wants to say no. He wants to pull away and tell Madison that Skylar and her parents would be waiting for him. But the thought of a sit-down dinner with his girlfriend's parents suddenly fills his stomach with dread. He looks at Madison's beautiful face. Then looking at her smiling soft lips, he feels a rush of desire that was like a drug, making him lose all control.

"Go on, son, the world is yours," came the Southern voice of Mason's antagonistic counselor. "How long do you think the other one is going to stay with you anyway? I know you've seen the way she looks at Chase. It's only a matter of time before she leaves you. Seize this opportunity." Wesley smirks, tips his hat at Madison even though, of course, she couldn't see him, and disappears behind her.

Images of Skylar with Chase suddenly flood Mason's mind. Earlier that day, he saw how Skylar laughed at something Chase whispered in her ear and then put her arm around him. Thinking back on the memory, his mind reimagines it to be a more flirtatious exchange than it really was. Skylar's words after Madison's audition come back to him as well: "If you want to take a break from us and explore what it is like to be a director with women throwing themselves at your feet, now is the time…" In reality, Mason knows that Skylar's words aren't meant to give permission for an unfaithful indiscretion. But, combined with Wesley's words, Mason chooses to interpret Skylar's suggestion for some time apart as indifference toward their relationship.

Turning his focus back at Madison, she is all he could see. Her smell, her skin, her touch, and suddenly, nothing else matters. Madison takes his hand and pulls Mason back into the Plaza Hotel. The doors of the elevator barely had enough time to close before Madison pushes Mason against the wall and presses her lips and body against his.

The Jacksons arrived at Avra and realize that Mason isn't there. Skylar tries calling him, but he doesn't answer. After thirty minutes, Skylar and her parents decided to sit at a table and begin ordering.

"Maybe he got caught up discussing *The Remake* and hasn't looked at his phone," Mrs. Jackson suggests.

"It's so unlike him. I hope he is okay," Skylar says.

"I'm sure he's fine and will show up any minute," Mr. Jackson adds to reassure his daughter.

The Jacksons order exotic cocktails and the beet salad for an appetizer. They each choose which fish they want cooked from the ice table with raw fish. The food is spectacular. Skylar tries to enjoy the branzino she orders, but in the pit of her stomach, she feels a sense of doom settling in as she continues worrying about Mason.

Just as they are about to order dessert, Mason walks through the door.

"I'm so sorry. My phone ran out of battery, and I didn't have a charger with me. I was about to head over here and then one of the managers from the Plaza said there was an issue with the bill, and we had to go over everything. How was dinner?"

Skylar is tempted to ask more questions about the bill and why he didn't use another phone to call her, but she feels uncomfortable having such a discussion in front of her parents. So the rest of the evening is spent getting to know each other. Mr. and Mrs. Jackson ask about Mason's upbringing, and he describes Peaks Island and playing hockey in Maine. He tells them that he was raised by his mother and grandparents in a loving home but left out the part about Hannah working as a medium. Instead, he just says she is in real estate.

As they head home, Mrs. Jackson calls her daughter to say that Mason seems very nice and that she and Mr. Jackson are happy for her. Skylar thanks them for coming to New York and says that she can't wait to see them again. The entire evening though, Skylar can't shake the feeling that something is wrong. Mason seemed a little odd during dinner, and at some point when she makes eye contact with him, Mason quickly shifts his gaze.

CHAPTER 10

HEARTACHE 1

Yet each man kills the thing he loves
By each let this be heard
Some do it with a bitter look
Some with a flattering word
The coward does it with a kiss
The brave man with a sword
—Oscar Wilde, *The Ballad of Reading Gaol*

The next day, Skylar is sipping her morning coffee on the balcony of her apartment when the doorman rings her on the phone to say that Chase Zacharias is in the lobby.

"Yes, let him up," Skylar says and hangs up the phone. She quickly runs into the bedroom and throws on a pair of jeans and plain black T-shirt. Then she hurries back into the kitchen to put her plate from breakfast in the dishwasher and wipes down the table. Just as she finishes, the knock comes on the door.

Chase looks handsome. He is an attractive guy, no doubt. His eyes are hazel and his hair a medium brown. His cheeks are soft, giving him a boyish charm.

"Hi, Skylar," Chase says sheepishly, looking at her and then down at his shoes. He isn't smiling, and Skylar realizes that he is there to tell her something that makes him feel uncomfortable. Being a beautiful young lady, it isn't the first time a guy showed up at her door to confess his feelings for her.

"Hey, this is a surprise. How's it going?" she says, trying to lighten the mood.

"Listen, I need to talk to you. I was up half the night deciding if I should even come by here but realize I have no choice but to let you know…"

"Wait, Chase. Look, Mason and I have been together a long time, and I really care about him a lot. I've loved working together and consider you a close friend but…"

"No, Skylar. You misunderstood. That's not what I came here to say."

"Oh. Oh my god, I'm so sorry." Skylar starts laughing. "That's so embarrassing!"

"Skylar. I do like you. I care about you and consider you a close friend too. Last night, as I was leaving the Plaza, I saw Mason." Chase takes a pause.

"What do you mean you *saw* him? We all saw him."

"I mean, after you left. Mason was with Madison. They were in the elevator together and… I saw them kissing."

Skylar feels her heart drop to the floor. As the image of Mason with Madison in an intimate embrace enters her mind, she feels nauseated. She walks away from Chase and sits down in the family room. Chase follows and sits next to her.

"I'm sorry, Skylar. I like you too much to let you go on thinking Mason is someone that he is not. It's better you know now rather than later."

She knows Mason has some emotional issues. Skylar remembers the anger in him when his mother announced her engagement, how jealous he was when they first met Chase, how he would get a sudden blank look on his face unexpectedly, like right after their first kiss. She recalls how he angrily tossed a bottle in the ocean and pushed James. Although she worries about his reactions sometimes, Skylar still loves Mason. She never thought he would cheat on her. They have been through so much together since first meeting on the train. How could he do this to her?

Skylar thinks that she would have cried, but the tears aren't coming. Even though she feels the deep ache in her heart, there is something else inside her telling her that she should have known. The signs were there all along. And last night, she actually thought that Mason might propose, but he was so late... and now she knows why. How could she have been so foolish? She wants to hide her pain from Chase. She looks at the handsome young man in her home and says, "I'm going to be okay, Chase. I'll get over this."

"I know you will, Skylar." Skylar could tell that Chase wanted very much to kiss her. She tactfully turns her gaze away from him, and instead he asks, "Do you want to go out and get a coffee somewhere? It sometimes helps just to go out and see people being busy."

"Thanks, Chase. But I think I need some time alone right now. Plus, at some point Mason is going to call me, and I have to confront him."

"Okay. I'll go, but if you need anything, just call."

After Chase leaves, Skylar picks up the phone. "Mason, we need to talk."

The tears come. They come suddenly and full force with the confrontation of his betrayal. Skylar shouts at Mason, "How could you do this! You are a liar! Don't ever call me again!" She hangs up the phone without giving Mason a chance to explain.

Mason doesn't call back. Skylar understands that his failure to defend himself is a verification of his guilt, and there is no fixing this relationship. She wipes her tears and grabs her purse to get out for some fresh air. Skylar walks aimlessly the rest of the day. When she finally sits on a park bench, she picks up her phone and sees the numerous texts from friends congratulating her on the success of *The Remake* premier. How bittersweet. Her heart aches over what happened with Mason and stifles the joy she wants desperately to feel with the success of her film. Why did this new beginning have to come with a tragic twist?

HEARTACHE 2

Mason stares at his phone in disbelief over what had happened. It feels like something is crawling on his skin, and he wants to get away from himself but can't. He plops down and closes his eyes, realizing the damage is done and there isn't anything he can do to fix it. How Skylar found out about Madison didn't matter. He realizes that he doesn't want to fix it because he loves Skylar and knows she deserved better.

Then Mason's phone rings. He saw the name on the caller ID: Madison Harper. Mason answers the phone, "Hey."

"Hi, Mason, I wish you didn't have to run off like that last night. Can you come over?"

With that, Mason feels a numbness come over him. He decides that he would do what he wants with whomever and whenever he wants. Mason is surprised by his own sudden indifference over what happened with Skylar, but his future lies ahead. His big, bright, successful future as a director means that he would be in command. He doesn't allow himself to succumb to heartbreak over his first love.

"There will be more like Skylar," he lies to himself.

CHAPTER 11

WHATEVER IT TAKES

No evil dooms us hopelessly except the evil we love, and desire to continue in, and make no effort to escape from.
—George Eliot, *Daniel Deronda*

*T*he *Remake* is hugely successful, and Mason appears at every event with Madison at his side. Their relationship is on display for the public. Madison doesn't hold back showing physical affection for Mason in public. The two of them show up to every event impeccably dressed and always pulling up in a fancy car, which had become somewhat of a hobby for Mason. He goes from splurging on a Maserati Gran Turismo to trading it in after a few months for a Bugatti Veyron. Mason buys himself a Tag Heuer Monaco watch, at a price of $47,000, making

Anthony and James's $6,400 Tag Heuer Carrera watches unimpressive in comparison. Madison indulges in Versace gowns that cost over ten thousand dollars each. Although this becomes somewhat of a cause for dispute between them as Madison would often overindulge in alcohol and spill cocktails on her gowns. Her sloppiness annoys Mason greatly even though he himself has lost dignity dabbling in drugs at parties.

One uncomfortably hot summer night, as a valet driver is pulling up the Bugatti Veyron, Mason warns Madison about her sloppy drinking. "Take it easy, Madison. No one is going to want to work with you if they think you're an irresponsible drunk."

Madison giggles, and her only reply is a loudly slurred "I just love this car!" as she rolls herself over the hood of the extravagant vehicle in her $8,900 vintage 1982 Versace silk starfish-and-seashell-themed gown with beaded bustier. She obnoxiously rolls over on her front side and begins to grind the hood of the car as if she is making love to it. And as she does so, the beads on her bustier slightly mark the car.

Mason has been watching her frustrated and embarrassed, but he sees the damage to his car immediately. "What the fuck, Madison! Get off my damn car!" And with that, he pulls her violently off the car.

Madison trips and falls down, scrapping her hand on the concrete. As the blood shown bright red on the pad of her hand, just below her wrist, Mason just stares at her. A slight tinge of compassion is quickly replaced with disgust. He wants to feel sorry for her, but he just can't. In Mason's opinion, she is a mess of her own making. There is nothing to pity in a person who can make such a fool of herself.

As a woman watching runs over to help Madison, she shouts at Mason, "What's wrong with you!"

For a few more seconds, Mason just watches Madison in her state of disgrace before he enters his Bugatti and puts the car in reverse. He looks at the women once more, and she and Madison looks at him in disbelief that he is going to just drive away…but that is exactly what Mason did.

"Call Skylar," Mason says calmly as the Bluetooth hand-free device in his car states, "Calling Skylar."

Over the last year, Mason has been keeping a close watch on the tabloids, searching for information on Skylar. He scans the social media pages of their mutual friends, hoping to catch a glimpse of her and what she's been up to…or, more specifically, with whom she's been with. He is able to piece together that Skylar has been asked to write and help direct one season of a show filmed in Chicago. Her work revives the show, and Mason sees pictures of her celebrating its success back home in Soho with friends. He examines her eyes in the photos to see any speck of heartbreak, but if there is any, it isn't evident in any pictures. Much to his relief, she isn't with any one particular guy on a repeated basis. Mason is relieved that she appears to be focused on her career.

Mason wonders if Skylar sees him with Madison, recklessly flaunting their relationship in tabloid magazines. Did it give her a carving sensation in her chest? Did she allow herself to really feel it or swallow it down like he did? How would she react to seeing his name appear on her ringing phone screen after all this time?

On the third ring, Skylar answers the phone, "Hello?"

"Skylar, thank God you answered. I have to see you."

"Mason? Uhmm, I wasn't expecting a call from you. See me? Why, Mason? I don't think I want to see you. I mean, I *know* I don't want to see you."

It pains him to hear her say those words to him. *She hates me,* he thinks to himself.

"Skylar, I'm sorry. I'm really, really, sorry. I love you. Please, try and understand that I was just overtaken by our success at the premier…"

"That's right, Mason…*our* success. *Our* success for *our* film that we worked so hard to make as a couple, and you threw it all away. You threw away the success we could have shared together and solidified our going our separate ways when you decided to give that night to Madison. You gave her what was ours, and you can't fix it. What you did…it was a sin against my soul. I will have to deal with this for the rest of my life."

He can't breathe. He never thought that he could really hurt someone that much, especially Skylar.

"I know I was wrong, but, please, don't say I can't fix it. I will find a way, just give me a chance. Please, Skylar."

"The answer is no, and it will always be no. Don't call me again, Mason. Goodbye."

Mason can hear her heavy breathing and knows that she is crying. He scrambles for words...

"Wait! Skylar? Hello?" But then the city background noise from the other end of the line goes silent.

"Fuck!" Mason slams his hand on the steering wheel.

Suddenly, a puff of cigar smoke invades his space, and when Mason looks over, he sees Wesley sitting in the passenger seat next to him.

"My boy. Boy, oh, boy. Women. That's just what they do. They expect us to be chained to them for the rest of our lives, and if we take a breath somewhere new, they will try and suck the life out of us. Listen to me, aah know you. You and aah are family. Aah know what is in your heart because it's in my heart too. Aah know it hurts. But it doesn't have to. There are ways to make that pain go away."

Mason continues driving and listening to Wesley. Wesley takes another puff of his cigar, and after slowly exhaling the fragrant smoke, he goes on, "Your next film, Mason. It's time to make another film. This time, let's write a ghost story."

Mason continues driving, not saying a word. He opens the windows of the Bugatti Veyron, letting in the hot air and letting out Wesley's cigar smoke. He looks straight ahead and continues to drive, not turning once to see Wesley. The heat from outside begins to create beads of sweat on his forehead. He feels a strange desire of wanting to be consumed by the heat. He wants his heartache to be taken over by something else. The reality he has been ignoring for so many months is in full view: he lost Skylar. He loves Skylar, and there is no way he can get her back now. He despises himself for what he had done, and he never wants to feel this way again. He never wants to love and screw it up again. Mason is ready to embrace Wesley's advice completely.

The ghost continues his general description of a potential movie plot in his casual, slow Southern drawl.

"A young woman returns to her small hometown to visit her parents from whom she has been estranged fo over a decade. After a while, she begins to notice strange things that don't seem quite right. Her parents don't look like they aged at all. Her bedroom was left exactly the same as when she was a ten-year-old girl. Then a neighborhood boy stops by, and she sees that he was her childhood friend who hasn't aged at all, either. And so forth and so on until it is revealed that the town had been buried under an avalanche, and all the people had died ten years ago."

Mason pulls into his Manhattan building's parking garage and parks the Bugatti. He took the elevator upstairs to his penthouse condo. Once inside, Mason goes to his bedroom and begins unbuttoning and then peeling off his shirt, which is wet with sweat. His expression is blank, and the pain in his chest is subsiding with his acceptance of his fate as a man rejected by love and the never-ending presence of the ghosts around him. Wesley is driving his actions now.

"Wait. Here is an idea. Call up that pretty actress you spotted at Cipriani Restaurant the other night. You know, the one who came up to you and said she wanted to work for you someday. Call her and tell her you already finished writing the script for your next film and are considering which actress would be a good fit for the lead role. What was her name? Zara, right?"

Mason stops undressing. He looks directly at Wesley, and without saying a word, Wesley knows that Mason understands what he planned.

Mason walks over to his computer and types in "Zara actress in New York." There she is. Zara's headshot appears and her agent's contact info. Mason calls the agent and arranges for Zara to meet him that same night.

After two hours or so, Zara is at Mason's door.

Once the door is opened, Zara smiles at Mason and shakes his hand, introducing herself again. With blondish hair, brown eyes, and a wide, full smile, Zara has classic movie star good looks with a practiced firm handshake.

"Zara, come in and have a seat."

Mason looks disheveled. He is wearing only a white undershirt over his dress pants, and his hair is messy. His skin looks worn and tired. Yet his eyes are glazed and intense. Is he on something, or are these the eyes of a bright director brimming with new ideas? He knows that Zara wouldn't be able to tell the difference. She is just a naive young woman desperate for work.

As Zara has a seat on the dark-gray sofa, Mason tells her about the script he just wrote, the ghost story suggested by Wesley.

"I think you might be right for the part of the main character. But I'm not sure yet. Why don't you come sit a little bit closer to me so I can get a better look at you?"

Mason can see she is taken back and appears frozen with his request. She appears uncertain as to where to focus her gaze, and he can tell her body stiffened. He imagines her heartbeat racing. Then Mason moves in directly toward her. He immediately puts his hands on her thighs and moves them upward as his lips forcefully meet hers. Zara sits there, and with trembling courage, she says, "Mason, please. I'm not ready for this. I just wanted to audition for the movie."

Mason pauses and looks at her intently. Somewhere, in the back of his mind, Mason knows that he is about to cross a line, there is no returning from. But that thought is buried so far away it is barely a whisper. He wants to feel pleasure and power to take away his pain...even transfer some of his pain to someone else. Mason can tell that Zara is shocked by the fierceness in his eyes and that it made her heart race faster.

"I can give the part to someone else, if you want." Then he smiles slyly and kisses her again.

If Zara knew that she should leave, if she told herself to get up and go, Mason makes sure to move so fast upon her that her thoughts would be mangled and buried, like his own.

CHAPTER 12

THE DIRECTOR

We must all suffer from one of two pains: the pain of discipline or the pain of regret. The difference is discipline weighs ounces while regret weighs tons.

—Jim Rohn

The next day, Zara's agent receives a call from Mason informing her that Zara got the part as the main character for his ghost story. The weeks go by while Mason completes writing the screenplay. Zara's agent lets her know that it is time to begin filming.

Zara tries to push aside what has happened between her and Mason by convincing herself it is normal and common in her profession. She tries to look at the incident as a hazing or price to pay for even greater success to come later. Mason would often send her flowers and invite her to private meetings in his hotel suite. She tries coming up with excuses for as long as she could, but eventually, Mason shows up at Zara's dressing room and demands that she meet with him.

"Zara, you are so pretty, and I just want to be with you. I know I came on a bit strong that first night, but you are just so irresistible. Please, have dinner with me tonight. I know the best chef in town, and when I ask him to, he prepares a special private dinner. I will call him right now…"

"Mason, I appreciate the role you gave me in your movie, but I don't want to have that kind of relationship with you." She pauses and then hopefully says, "Can we please keep this professional?"

Mason looks at Zara sternly. She knows that he would not accept no for an answer. Of course, she doesn't know that Wesley is a constant presence by his side now, convincing Mason to get his way at all costs to prove that he has the power and is in charge.

Presenting a calm demeanor, Mason says, "Zara, you are so pretty. This role is only for the most special of actresses. If you don't want to be that special actress, I can find someone else who does. Look, let's start over. Meet me tonight. I'll be waiting for you." He leans his broad, muscular shoulders in toward Zara and kisses her gently on the cheek, sending chills up and down her spine.

As filming continues the rest of the day, Zara tries to ignore what is waiting for her afterward. She still hasn't decided what she is going to do. An internal struggle is going on in her head. Of course, the moral high ground is to walk off that set and never look back. But then what? How would she find work as an actress after word got out that she just walked off a movie set and breached her contract? If she continues filming but didn't meet with Mason later, he would fire her and damage her reputation beyond repair. Or she could sell her soul to the devil by meeting him for dinner, doing as he asked, but then move on to her next film as an acclaimed actress. Then she could put all this behind her. She knows that her answer is clear: she doesn't actually have a choice.

Dreading the inevitable dinner, Zara pours herself into the role she is acting on set. By completely immersing herself into this other person, she can take the image of her with Mason out of the forefront of her mind. But sure enough, the hours and then the minutes go by, and the last take of the day is filmed. Zara says good night to the rest of the cast and starts walking off set. Mason walks up to her, smiles, and whispers, "Don't make me wait too long."

In her room, Zara puts on a dark red, silk, off-the-shoulder blouse with a pair of black jeans. Her high-heeled gray suede boots came just over her knees. She looks at herself in the mirror and decides that her outfit looks too provocative for this meeting. She switches the blouse for a long sleeve cotton green shirt with a simple V-neck. Instead of the boots, she opts for black sneakers. "Maybe he will realize what he did was wrong, and we could just eat dinner and call it a night," she tries desperately to convince herself.

At Mason's door, she knocks twice. Mason shouts, "It's open, come in!"

Zara looks down at her shoes and takes a deep breath before turning the knob and pushing open the door. She steps inside and closes the door behind her. The moment she turns around, the music begins playing loudly, it is "Faded Heart" by Borns, and out steps Mason, wearing only his jeans and a purple feather boa.

The lyrics begin immediately, and Mason starts singing along. He imitates the high-pitched sound of the singer's voice, and his dancing is so unexpected. Zara couldn't tell if he is channeling a young Mick Jagger or a drag queen. He sings along and then moves in toward Zara with a smile and crazed look on his face. Then he slips a pill into her mouth. Frozen, she just swallows it. Mason goes on, dancing with hips swaying and shoulders moving side to side as his hands come to his heart, and his face shows anguish and pleasure all at once as he continues singing.

Not sure what strange universe she entered into, Zara begins to see images of Parisian cabaret cancan dancers dancing in sync with Mason. Is it the pill she just swallowed? As much as Zara does not want to appear to be having a good time, this is very amusing, and she lets out a little laugh. Zara realizes that Mason takes the term "doesn't give a shit" to a whole other level.

The man does whatever he feels like doing with unparalleled intensity. In this bizarre dance show where Mason is the lead dancer in an array of feathers and topless leggy Parisian girls dancing faster, the song goes on, and then Mason pushes himself up against Zara and grabs her body closer to his. She knows that she has been hallucinating the dancing girls, and now the lights start to dim as well. Zara feels herself relax, and her mind starts to drift off.

Zara awakes in Mason's bed the next morning. She is naked with a black silk bedsheet pulled over her body. Frightened at the realization that she has no recollection of what has happened or how she got where she is, she quickly sits up. Her head is spinning, and she sees Mason asleep beside her. Zara quietly gets up, gets dressed, and leaves the room without waking Mason.

It is past dawn, and the heat from the day before continues into a muggy morning. Zara hails a taxi, and in less than an hour, she is back in her own room. Zara thinks about what had happened the night before. She remembers laughing at Mason dancing and the wild look in his eyes. But that was it. Something did happen afterward though, of that she is certain. The thought of going on set in just a few hours sends her head spinning and pounding. In her kitchen cabinet, she takes out two Tylenol and swallows them with an icy glass of water mixed with salt and lemon, remembering someone who told her it would help with dehydration and replace lost electrolytes.

Defeated, scared, ashamed, and exhausted. If this is what it takes to be an actress, Zara knows that she couldn't do it. How many Mason Hunters are out there? What strange abuse would she have to face to land a role? All she wants to do is get in bed, hide under her covers, and stay there forever. The day ahead, facing Mason again, is unbearable. That's when she decides that she would call in sick and visit the only person she could think of who might be able to help her.

Zara has read the tabloid stories about Mason's betrayal of Skylar. Over the course of the last year, Skylar has earned a reputation of being a fair and respected young director. Zara knows that if she goes to her friends or family, they would insist she calls the police. But Zara isn't ready to face the likely demise of her budding acting career that would follow if she reports what happened to authorities. No one would want to hire the actress who reported some kind of sexual assault by a director. Worse, she couldn't remember what exactly happened last night. Maybe Skylar can help her find a way out of her contract with Mason. *Then Skylar can help me find another role somewhere,* Zara thinks to herself.

CHAPTER 13

A LACE MASK

We must take sides. Neutrality helps the oppressor, never the victim. Silence encourages the tormentor, never the tormented.

—Elie Wiesel

In the same Soho apartment where she lived since film school, Skylar is brewing her morning coffee. Her Fitbit watch begins to vibrate with a notification that she is receiving a call from an unknown number. She opens her purse, pulls out her iPhone, and answers, "This is Skylar."

"Hi, Skylar. My name is Zara. I have been filming a movie with Mason Hunter and..." Zara begins sobbing uncontrollably.

"Hello? Are you okay?" Skylar moves her hair away and pushes her phone closer to her ear as she tries to figure out what is going on.

Sniffling, Zara goes on, "Yes. I mean, no. No, I'm not okay." After a pause for several seconds, Zara manages to say it out loud, "Mason Hunter is a fucking rapist!"

Skylar is shocked. She isn't sure what to say or do next. "What? Mason? A rapist? I'm sorry, but I dated Mason for a long time, and although he can be a jerk sometimes, I'm having a hard time believing he would do something like that."

"He raped me! I had no idea he was such a monster. I just thought he was handsome, and I was actually attracted to him, but I didn't expect him to do what he did to me. I mean, Mason is a successful director and in a relationship with Madison Harper. I don't know how to deal with this! He was just so much stronger than me, and I was so scared. I was scared to even try and fight him. I thought if I fought back, it would only make him angry and more violent. Then, last night it happened again. I can't even remember what he did to me! I don't know what to do. I just want to be an actress. If I go to the police and they can't prove he did it, I'll never find work anywhere. My acting career will be over. I can't let that happen, I've wanted to be an actress my whole life." Zara stops and waits, but there is no response on the other end.

Skylar isn't sure what to say. She doesn't know Zara, and this stranger is making very serious and shocking accusations against Mason.

After a few seconds of silence, Zara declares, "I don't know why I called you. I shouldn't have bothered. Look, forget I called. Don't say anything to anyone, please."

"Wait." Skylar tries to stop her, but Zara has already hung up.

Gathering her thoughts, Skylar knows that she has to confront Mason. Could he have attacked that actress somehow? How is it possible when he never showed any aggression toward her all the years they were together? Is it a hoax or some setup for blackmail? Either way, there is no way she could ignore what Zara told her.

Once she decides to go see Mason, Skylar dashes out of her apartment as fast as she could and hails a taxi for Manhattan. As soon as she arrives at Mason's building, the doorman recognizes her and lets her up immediately. She knocks on Mason's door.

CHAPTER 14

MONSTER MASON

There are hunters, and there are victims. By your discipline, cunning, obedience, and alertness, you will decide if you are a hunter or a victim.

—Jim Mattis

Mason slowly opens his eyes. He rolls over and sees that no one is there. His head feels stuffy, and for a moment he isn't sure if last night really happened. But the memories all come back, and he knows for certain what he had done. Mason opens the drawer of his dresser to grab clean underclothes and inside is his grandfather's watch. It has been there for so long it had almost become invisible. But now, the face of the watch stares at him, and Mason realizes that he has grown into a completely different man compared to the honest and humble grandfather he had loved. He angrily shuts the drawer and pushes away his feelings of inadequacy and failure.

There is more knocking. Is that his door?

He goes to the door, and without asking who is there, Mason opens it, looking drowsy and hungover. But as soon as he realizes it is Skylar, he perks up.

"Skylar. I wasn't expecting to see you. Come in." The sight of her gorgeous dark eyes and smooth skin is so comforting. Mason still longs for her touch, but Skylar walks past Mason and into the condo but then notices a spilled drink on the coffee table. There is lipstick on the glass that lays sideways on the pale gray rug. Mason follows Skylar's eyes as she looks behind the couch and sees the bar that looks like someone has smashed something, or someone, at it…there are bottles knocked over and pieces of broken glass everywhere. Skylar stops walking further and takes a step back.

"Mason, an actress just called me saying that you did something really terrible to her. What happened?"

"Normal things happened, Skylar. That's all. She's just an actress looking to become famous. Just like all of them." Mason steps closer to Skylar, but she steps back. Agitated, Mason says, "What was that? Are you afraid of me now?"

Skylar stands there, not moving, not saying anything. Mason is looking over her shoulder, and he starts speaking to someone else. "I will do whatever I want," Mason says.

Skylar looks behind her, no one she can see is there. "Mason, who are you talking to?" she asks with a quiver. The room becomes cold. It must have dropped several degrees.

"It's Wesley, my beautiful Skylar. It's just my dead great-great-grandfather," Mason replies with a laugh that was filled with anguish. "He says I should 'take you.' What do you think that means?" Then Mason pulls Skylar close to him, and she looks terrified.

"Mason, don't do this. If you think I'm going to keep it a secret that you attacked that actress, you're wrong. I won't keep any of this a secret. I will go straight to the police. You are a rapist! Let me go!" She tries to pull away from him, but he holds her tight.

"I'm much more than a rapist, Skylar." Mason moves his hands up around her throat. "You've left me no choice, Skylar. My beautiful love. But you betrayed me, you left me for Chase and broke my heart. I knew he was the one you really wanted to be with, and it tore me apart. This is the only way I can end this pain."

"No, you're so wrong, Mason…" Skylar tries to speak, but Mason squeezes her throat tighter.

Wesley stands only a few feet away, watching. "You're almost there, kid. You will be the most famous director the world has ever known."

Tears stream down Skylar's face.

"What do you see, Skylar? Flashes of your life? Do you see your parents smiling at you, your childhood home, playing hide-and-seek outside until dusk with cousins, family vacations at the beach…or are you praying to God for a miracle?"

Suddenly, Mason lets go. Skylar curls to her side and gasps for air.

Mason stares in disbelief as a woman appears wearing a long green dress in the style of the south in the 1920s. Initially, he couldn't figure out who or what this woman was doing here. Then he remembers Wesley's story from when they first met and knows that it is Charlotte.

CHAPTER 15

CHARLOTTE

Once you drop a mask, you can never wear it again.

—Anthon St. Maarten

Charlotte's blue eyes look down at Skylar and then at Mason with disappointment and heartache. Then she looks at Wesley and speaks sternly. "You do not belong here. You have no place in this family."

"Charlotte," Wesley begins pleadingly, "I've searched everywhere for you. I found the desk William gave to you, and I knew Mason was part of our family."

"This is my family! This is mine, not yours! You do not belong here! Leave and don't ever come back!" And with a flick of her wrist, Wesley falls backward. With a shocked look on his face, Wesley says, "Please, Charlotte, don't leave me again, you were the best thing that ever happened to me in my life."

Mason can't believe Wesley looks so scared and weak. Is this the same person who spoke to him with such determined confidence these past few years? Wesley crawls towards Charlotte and touches the hem of her dress. "Please, spare me, Charlotte." Charlotte steps back and says, "Your evil deeds will always send you back into the darkness, there is no light in your heart." Suddenly, Charlotte raises her arms and creates a ball of light between her hands. "Charlotte! No, please!" he begins to plead but his expression quickly changes to one of rage and he gets up to charge at Charlotte, but she throws her arms at him and he is pushed back down and disappears.

"Who are you?" Mason asks. "What are you doing in my place? I didn't summon any ghosts here!" Mason tries to get up, but he is weak and angry. As tears stream down his face, he tries to use his energy to make the ghost disappear by shouting at her to leave, but he couldn't.

Charlotte moves in closer to Mason. "You can't force the spirits who love you to leave, Mason. You cannot push away your family. You may have been able to push away Wesley when you wanted him to leave, but that's because *he* is not your family. *I* am."

"How could that be? Wesley is my great-great-grandfather. We are so similar, he and I. He was helping me." Mason stops talking when he realizes what he is saying. What exactly was Wesley helping him do? Why and when did Mason start listening to Wesley's crazy thoughts?

"Listen to me, Mason. I am your great-great-grandmother. And after all that has happened here, I have to tell you my story."

Charlotte puts her hand on Mason's shoulder, and the two of them are transported to a different place and time. This time, Mason finds himself in a large theater unlike any he has been to before. There is a large stage and orchestra pit. The auditorium is fan shaped and seated at least three thousand people. The opulent theater is also multileveled and the decor ornate and luxurious.

"Welcome to the Strand Theatre in Brooklyn, New York. It opened in 1914, and I was just a young girl then. My parents brought me here to see various performances, and it became my obsession. Initially, the theater was built for vaudeville, but a few years later, it was converted to a movie theater. I wanted to see every movie playing at this picture palace. Being in here, I felt that anything was possible. How could one not feel that way? When a person could build such a majestic architectural masterpiece, you feel that people can really do anything. Uniformed employees guided visitors to the grand lobby, up a sweeping staircase, down wide promenades, into this incredible auditorium.

"I knew I wanted to be on that screen someday. Then I learned about Gladys Louise Smith. She was known professionally as Mary Pickford. Mary Pickford was an actress and producer. She cofounded both the Pickford-Fairbanks Studio and the United Artists film studio. In the 1910s and 1920s, Mary

Pickford was one of the most popular actresses and earned the nickname 'Queen of the Movies.'"

As Charlotte and Mason sit in the theater seats, the screen begins to play a movie of the story that Charlotte is telling. Each scene unfolds before them as Charlotte tells her tale.

"I told my father I wanted to be just like Mary Pickford. He found it amusing until I came of age, and he realized I was serious. My father didn't think it was practical or becoming of a young woman to aspire to be an actress and would not allow me to enroll in any acting classes. I lied to my parents and joined a local theater group. When my father found out, he was furious and sent me to stay with my cousin, Grace, on a plantation in Charleston, South Carolina, far away from the Strand Theatre.

"The first evening with Grace, William, and Wesley, I knew Wesley was smitten with me. He stared wide-eyed as I played the piano and sang for them that night. Wesley would often invite me to stroll the plantation with him, and although it was pretty, it was hot, uncomfortable, and mosquito ridden. But there wasn't much else to do when the sun went down, and I agreed.

"Wesley and I were friends until one unusually hot night in October, when we heard jazz music playing. I loved to dance, and Wesley joined me for several hours. We had a couple of drinks, and as we were getting ready to leave, Wesley pulled me behind the cabin. He forced himself on me, and I became pregnant.

"I wanted to go back home to New York, but William and Grace insisted we get married to protect my reputation. In those days, women didn't have many choices or rights. Women couldn't buy land or even have their own bank account. William and Grace wouldn't allow me to live with them and disgrace the family with a child out of wedlock. I tried telling Grace in private that Wesley forced himself on me, but she insisted that men normally react that way when a young lady is overly flirtatious. I had nowhere else to go but with Wesley. With a heavy heart, I accepted when Wesley gave me his mother's onyx ring. Strange but fitting my sadness, Wesley didn't know onyx stones are usually worn by women in mourning. Within a few days, we were set to travel to Boston a couple engaged to be married.

"We traveled by train to Boston. I was eating braised duck Cumberland in the dining parlor when a young man approached Wesley and I. He introduced himself as Adrian Blake, and our connection was immediately and mutually felt. As Adrian discussed his idea for a movie, I realized I could not take another bite. When Adrian hinted that he might cast me for the leading role, I felt a sudden exhilaration after weeks of despair with Wesley.

"Later that evening, I became violently ill. The braised duck I had eaten earlier caused food poisoning. With the combination of the bumpy train ride and food poisoning, I miscarried. Thankfully, a doctor on the train tended to me, and after a day or so, I regained some of my strength. Wesley was devastated with the loss. He was angry too.

"Eventually, we arrived at the gorgeous Palmer House in Chicago. It was in the hotel, between two-winged statue candelabras, that I met my dear friend, Farah. Farah told me about the Women's World Fair in Chicago, and soon we made plans to go together. At the Women's Fair, on April 18, 1925, we heard Lillian Tolbert's speech about how she devised a new kind of pitcher that kept ice separate in the core to keep drinks cold, the Tolbert Pitcher. Ms. Tolbert beamed as she explained that the only man who had anything to do with her invention was the attorney at the patent office. Farah and I began discussing the possibility that a movie could be written, directed, and produced entirely by women. I talked about Mary Pickford and said that we could be like her someday. Farah and I became good friends with Lillian and enjoyed ourselves in the city as often as we could.

"Since I had been living with Wesley for some time by then as a couple engaged to be married, we finally tied the knot during a blizzard in 1924. On our wedding night, Adrian, Farah, Lillian, Wesley, and I danced for hours. At the end of the evening, I suggested our entire group join for a sleepover in the master bridal suite. I was thankful not to have to fake intimacy with Wesley, and Adrian and I exchanged more than a few tender caresses that night after the rest of the group fell asleep. I did not love Wesley. I was in love with Adrian. I was unfaithful to my husband, the man who had raped me, and spent long wonderful afternoons in the arms of my true love, Adrian. When I became pregnant with Adrian's child, I lied and told Wesley the baby was his.

"You must understand, Mason, that in those days, this was the only way. A women's reputation was crucial to her success, and an affair was blasphemy and beyond repair. Nonetheless, I think Wesley knew that the child wasn't his. Soon after I announced my pregnancy, Wesley suggested Farah try out for a part in Adrian's movie, which Wesley was producing. Farah got the part but thereafter became rather quiet and different somehow. When I pushed her to tell me what was wrong, she bravely explained how Wesley invited her to a private audition and then asked her to give him a massage, which made her very uncomfortable. She reluctantly obliged, hoping it was an innocent gesture, but then Wesley forced himself upon her. Of course, I knew she was telling the truth from my own experiences with Wesley.

"As the months passed, Wesley directed several films and became rather famous. Adrian and I continued to see each other in secret, but Wesley must have suspected something was going on as he began to reject every script from Adrian. Since we were no longer working together, it became harder to see each other. Wesley circulated rumors that Adrian was an alcoholic, and soon he couldn't get work anywhere. These were difficult times for us. It was heartbreaking for me to watch Adrian struggle to find work after being the reason behind Wesley's success.

"My beautiful Clara was born, and I had to continue to work. I couldn't rely on Wesley to care for us as he would disappear for days, and the rumors of his aggressive behavior toward women continued to grow. I dreaded seeing Wesley during this time and tried to keep Clara away from him as much as possible. I had our nanny constantly take Clara on excursions."

Charlotte takes a deep inhale and sighs remembering what came soon after in her life. The screen goes black. Mason sits in the theater chair and waits. "Please, go on," he says quietly. Next, on the screen, there slowly illuminates a jazz band.

"The Pickwick Club in Boston. It was July 3, 1925. This had always been my favorite time of year. The weather was warm, and everyone was outside enjoying themselves late into the evening, as the following day was Independence Day, and every citizen of our great country celebrated our national holiday. The days were long and filled with frequent trips to the beach. But on that day, as McGlennon's jazz orchestra played, Adrian and I found ourselves on the dance floor facing each other and began to dance. Suddenly, we no longer cared who saw our display of love. We danced faster and faster into a hurricane of heat. I saw Wesley angrily watching us, but I didn't care. I wanted nothing more to do with him. In my mind, I was determined to live a life with Adrian and Clara anywhere far away from Wesley.

"Suddenly, it felt like sand was falling on our heads, and we quickly realized that something was wrong with the building. Adrian and I rushed toward the exit, but Wesley came at us. He hit Adrian unconscious with a two by four. Then he looked at me. He dropped his weapon and then hit me with the back of his hand, knocking me unconscious as well. Adrian and I weren't able to escape as the building collapsed completely. The love of my life and my dear friends were among the forty-four people who died that night. We were so close to happiness, but Wesley made sure we never lived to see that day.

"Rather than raising my daughter as her mother, I became her guardian angel. I was always there in spirit, in a way that you cannot understand, Mason. I have been watching over you as well, child. Everyone feels lost at some point in their lives. Not sure who we are anymore and who we are meant to be or what our purpose is. But what Wesley led you to believe, that you come from someone violent, like him, is a lie. A lie that almost had devastating consequences. That is not you, Mason. Not now, not ever."

Mason feels his eyes fill with tears that run hot down his face. He leans in to embrace Charlotte, but before he can touch her, it all disappears. Suddenly, Mason is back in his apartment with Skylar on the floor, still gasping for air as if only a moment has passed.

"Skylar, I am so sorry. I don't know what happened to me. It was like I was possessed. I am so sorry."

Skylar looks at him and, with her throat aching, manages to push out the words: "Mason, you hurt me. You hurt Zara. You hurt us in a way you can never make right."

"I will make it right. I have to."

CHAPTER 16

THE MORNING AFTER

Bad habits are spiraling slides that drag you round and round down the narrowing end of a cone that eventually ends up in a dark, tight, confining spot.

—Richelle E. Goodrich

M uch to Mason's surprise, Skylar does not rush out of his apartment that horrible night when he almost killed her. She stays close and even held him in her arms until dawn. Mason wants to believe that Skylar still cares deeply for him despite his crimes. Could anyone love him after what he did? Does he even deserve love? Was he *ever* even worthy of another person's love? Those questions loom in his mind when Skylar slowly releases her arms from around him and stands up. They look into one another's eyes but do not say a word. Mason does not have any words for her. Even "thank you" is not appropriate. After searching her face for compassion but seeing only uncertainty, confusion, and disappointment, he watches Skylar turn and walk out of the room. He listens intently as the door opened and then closed slowly.

Mason sits motionless and quiet on the sofa as if he is the victim instead of the other way around. If Skylar decides to call the police, he knows that his career would be over, and there isn't anything he could do about it. So he just waited.

This day ends in silence the way it began. Mason cannot bring himself to turn on the television. He does not listen to music or read any books. He wanders through his home, pacing, pacing until he is tired and then lies down. The police do not come.

At least for now, it appears that Skylar chooses not to report his crimes, and neither does Zara. He knows that Zara probably never reported the incident to any official authority because she didn't want the negative publicity that could hurt her career. But why didn't Skylar call the police?

On the following day, Mason awakes to his phone ringing. It was Skylar.

"Hello?"

"Zara and I will take over directing your film. You will not receive any credit for the movie. Zara is going to be my codirector in addition to playing the lead role. Call your lawyer and get all of this in writing by the end of the day. And, Mason, you need to get help. I want proof that you are going to start seeing a psychologist immediately."

"Um…" Mason clears his throat. "Of course, I will."

"Good," Skylar replies and then ends the call.

Mason follows Skylar's instructions. Over the next several months, the two women are working on his film, and he knows that he is not to receive any for it. During this time, Mason attends therapy sessions and learns a lot about himself and who he wants to be. He learns to forgive himself for what he had done to Zara and Skylar. However, there is something Mason would never discuss with his therapist: Wesley. He fears that this could lead to a psychiatric record labeling him as suffering from delusional insanity or even schizophrenia. When the therapist asks if he sees any images that aren't really there, or hallucinations, he simply denies it.

Mason spends a good amount of time researching psychological disorders that include "seeing ghosts" to make sure he does not hint at any such problem. Especially because medication to treat these conditions come with side effects that include drowsiness and blurred vision which would make Mason's intended return to the movie business impossible.

There is someone Mason knows that would be able to help him with the ghost problem, should Wesley ever reappear, and so he heads home to Peaks Island. Hannah and Anthony have been enjoying their engagement and rather than live entirely in Maine or Peaks Island, they decide to keep both homes and move from one house to the other as they wish. Knowing that Mason is coming to stay with her, Hannah asks that Anthony stay in Maine for a few weeks so that she can focus on her son.

Mason sits with his mother in the sunroom overlooking the backyard of the house on Peaks Island. It is winter now and bitter cold, but the sunroom is always Mason's favorite room of the house. Snow sparkles in the yard covering everything in white. To the left, one can see the steadfast ocean, always changing but always there. Hannah lights the fireplace, and the two of them sit side by side on the sofa. Hannah wears a heavy shawl to keep her warm, and Mason throws a wool blanket over his shoulders.

"Mom, I can't believe what I've done." Mason tells his mother what had transpired between him, Wesley, Charlotte, Skylar, and Zara.

"Mason, don't ever let yourself be fooled about who you are again. Wesley tricked you. By making a connection with you when he first appeared to you, he was able to begin building your trust. He appeared on his own in your bedroom as if he belonged there and said he wanted to help you. The desk in your room played a role in his scheme too. By saying it was sent by him, Wesley further established his connection to your life. He was able to begin building your trust and feeding on your weaknesses, your desire for acceptance, and your longing for a father figure.

"You need to have a firm connection in your heart and mind that your intentions are always good. At your center, there is love and no ill will toward others. Mason, you are in charge, and only you decide what can present itself to you. Every day, remind yourself and strengthen your belief in yourself by repeating this mantra, 'My mind is my own. My soul is my own. Only I can decide which thoughts enter my mind and which ones I demand to leave. I am in complete control of my mind and soul. I will only ever surrender myself to God almighty.'"

Mason wonders at how it is possible that his mother can so completely believe the things she just told him. He wishes he can believe too, life would be so much easier if he has her kind of blind faith. Unfortunately, he knows that he wouldn't be repeating Hannah's daily mantra. Then Hannah's expression changed…

"What? You look like you want to say something else…"

"There is something else you need to know, Mason. I saw Skylar and James together last week. They were having dinner together, just the two of them. I think it's important that you know and give yourself time to deal with the fact that it looks like they might be dating now."

Mason looks away and feels the heartache stab him and rise up to his throat. He stands up and begins pacing the room.

"Mason, are you okay?"

Mason quickly grabs whatever he can reach. The first thing is his cup of tea. He tosses it into the fireplace. It crashes and splashes, and Mason quickly turns to grab a pillow, but Hannah pulls it away from him. He lets go but then grabs another and tosses that into the fire.

"Mason, stop!" Hannah yells, but Mason grabs the centerpiece on the coffee table with both hands. It is a long ornamental candle votive holder. With both arms, he destroys the centerpiece in the fire. He is about to look for something else when he sees Hannah. She is standing with her face in her hands, and he knows that she is sobbing.

"It's okay, Mom. I'll be okay. I am going to move on from this. I already have an idea for my next movie. It's a story about a woman named Charlotte who visits her cousin in Charleston, South Carolina."

Raising her head from hands, Hannah looks at Mason, stunned. Mason knows that he frightens her. Now he knows that he has hurt everyone he loved. He looks around the room at the damage he caused and his mother's tear-streaked face. Cleaning this up wouldn't fix it, and his presence is only hurting Hannah more. So he left.

CHAPTER 17

SELF-LOATHING

I have tried to drink this pain away,
to smoke it away,
to write it away.
I tried to make it numb,
I tried to run away from it,
I tried to fight it.
But everything I tried to escape
found me in my sleep
again.
—Mandy K., *The Final Stroke*

One year later

M ason decides to set his alarm on his iPhone to go off every day at 6:00 a.m. to begin his day with a workout, a shower, a protein shake, and some time to get his mind-set on the right path of self-motivation and overall positivity. But when it went off at 6:00 a.m., on a snow-covered morning in New York with its alarm set to the sound of "radar," he does not even bother to hit the snooze button. Instead, he just turns it off and sinks his head into his black silk pillowcase. He pulls the gray covers up to his chin and rolls over so as not to view anything of the outside world from his bedroom windows.

Overwhelming dread comes over him as he recalls the critics' reviews of "Charlotte." Some said it lacks a clear point of view, making it difficult for the audience to connect with the main character let alone any character. Others wrote that it "lacks vision and connection to real human relationships." Bad review after bad review coupled with a mediocre trailer led to the lowest ticket sales of any other movie playing at the box office. In other words, Mason produced his first film that completely bombed.

This realization makes Mason feel like crawling out of his own skin and escaping his own self. Since he has to use the washroom, he forces his body out of bed. Looking down, he sees his toned and fit physique. Thanks to weekly skin-pampering treatments, his skin is also perfect. Well-defined abs and biceps are created by almost daily visits from his personal trainer. His boxer shorts are ridiculously expensive because $225 for a pair of Derek Rose boxers wouldn't make a dent in his bank account that had seen royalties for months after the release of *The Remake*. But now he is facing a new reality that dims the light of his previous success to barely a flicker. He wants to escape, but alas, he is stuck with his newfound failure, and the gnawing pain of it is inescapable.

It has been almost a year since his heart-to-heart talk with Hannah in the four seasons room in his Peak Island childhood home. It was then that he first announced that he would write and produce a movie about his great-grandmother, Charlotte. In the months that followed, Mason devoted himself completely to writing the script, casting the right actors, choosing the settings, and directing *Charlotte*. He felt he had turned over a new leaf. Wesley was gone, and his weekly sessions with his psychiatrist helped him learn to let go of past anger, guilt, and resentment.

Now Mason's mind is rolling over memories of himself and the fervor with which he walked around the movie set, directing the crew. Images of his own carefree laughter and joy while creating an ode to Charlotte makes him cringe. He actually believed that the movie would be his masterpiece and redemption for the selfish monster he had been. How ridiculous the memories of himself filming during that time seem to him now.

The self-loathing he feels is growing unbearable. Mason wants to punish himself. Desiring to escape his own skin, Mason drags his nails down his arms, creating ugly, almost bloody red lines. His face distorts to an angry scowl, and like a trapped animal, Mason begins to destroy everything he could reach. He tears down the curtains and thrashes about the room, throwing down lamps and decorative items on his dresser. But his anger will not relinquish. He must redeem himself, but how?

Seeking to satisfy this madness, Mason's gaze moves to the prized paintings hanging on his wall. These are pricey works of art that Mason had carefully selected from new talent that he personally met with and felt a connection to, artistically speaking. Each painting brings back memories of talks with the artists who created them and how they looked up to Mason as he boasted about his professional success in the film industry.

Skylar suddenly appears in his memories. Mason knows that losing her is his greatest failure of all and stings the most. Since his split with Skylar, nothing has been as fulfilling as the time he spent with her. He must get her back. If only God could reach down and plant an idea in his head that will win back her love. He remembers days at museums, in parks, and best of all, in her room. Then the memory of that horrible night with Zara comes back to him as well, and he is filled with shame and disgust.

Overcome by his madness, Mason propels himself to the first painting. He pauses a moment to admire the striking waves of red, gold, and orange watercolor painted on the canvas by a doe-eyed bohemian artist. He pulls the painting upward, unhinging it from the wall, and with a swift motion, Mason brings it crashing down over his bedpost. Completely destroyed. One by one, Mason stops and examines the remaining two paintings in his bedroom before lifting them off the wall and bringing them crashing down in a final act of self-punishment for his failings.

He aches for something or someone to make him feel good. However, now that Mason is no longer at the top of his game, finding that easy someone ready to please him is not going to be as readily available. So instead, Mason walks down the hall of his penthouse apartment and into the kitchen. One wall houses a wine cellar, and inside there is a cabinet with a variety of vodkas, whiskeys, and gins. He goes for Tito's Vodka and pours some over rocks into a low glass. Sip after cold sip, the pain seems to slowly fade. After a second drink, Mason washes up, gets dressed, and calls an Uber driver to pick him and take him into town.

By now, it is midafternoon. Mason walks through the cold streets with his winter coat, hat, hood, and sunglasses. No one will recognize him. Walking past art galleries only reminds him of what he just destroyed. He knows he will regret what he did to his artwork someday, but he does not care to think about that too much at the moment. Not sure where he is going or what he is looking for, Mason just keeps walking until he comes to a sign that reads "Reiki."

Mason mindlessly walks through the door that leads straight up a staircase. At the top of the stairs, he rings a bell shaped like a quarter moon. A middle-aged woman, short in stature, with intense-looking dark eyes, opens the door and asks, "Can I help you?"

"I saw your sign out front for Reiki."

"Do you have an appointment?"

"No."

She looks a tad bit annoyed but, after a pause, says, "All right. Come in and have a seat while I get the room ready."

Mason sits on a small sofa in a crammed living room. The walls are covered with pictures of people and gods and deities that Mason has never seen before.

"Here, drink a glass of water and come with me."

She leads Mason around the corner where a massage table awaits behind a curtain dividing it from a tiny kitchen. This room is covered with similar pictures as well.

"Lay down on your back and just relax."

Mason lies down and closes his eyes. He briefly opens them only to see that the woman is simply waving her hands up and down his body and head just barely above his skin. He allows himself to relax and rest.

"Here, in your throat chakra. There is a lot of blockage. Everything is tangled up here. I will try to clear this."

This is his first time ever trying Reiki, and Mason isn't even sure what he is doing here other than he wants to just lie down and have someone take care of him for a little while. He could have gone to a spa for an expensive treatment, but this just seems easier right now. Plus, he had heard somewhere that Reiki helps people find their purpose in life, and he needs some direction right now.

Lying there with his eyes closed, Mason's mind keeps drifting back to Skylar, Zara, his mother, and then Charlotte. He feels a pain in his chest like he is about to cry. He tries to stifle it as best he could, but he can't hold back the tears, and he feels himself jerked upward as uncontrollable tears pour from his eyes, and his chest feels like it is going to split open.

The Reiki practitioner looks at him. "That needed to come out for some time now."

Mason lies back down, and the Reiki practitioner continues with her laying of the hands. Mason feels himself relax more and more. When the session is over, Mason sits up and feels lighter.

"Drink a lot of water and rest when you go home."

Mason pays her sixty dollars and heads home.

Back in his disaster of a bedroom, Mason begins to feel chills as if a fever were setting in. What is happening? He isn't feeling the new sense of purpose or clarity he had hoped to achieve when he entered the Reiki studio.

He begins to research "Reiki." After the initial Wikipedia articles and advertisements on learning how to become a Reiki practitioner or the benefits of Reiki, Mason finds an article titled, "The Hidden Dangers of Reiki." Mason's chest tightens as he reads more and more. The article discusses how Reiki practitioners prepare a room before seeing a client by calling up false gods. The practitioners claim that they heal by universal energy, but, in fact, the universal energy is an evil energy that can now easily enter the recipient willingly as he or she lays there unaware of what is really happening. Often, the article states, a Reiki practitioner will have pictures of false gods surrounding their room, and the practice is vehemently anti-Christian.

Mason clicks the back button and enters another search: "Is Reiki evil?"

As he scrolls through the headings of various articles, one in particular catch his attention. "Reiki Instructor Regrets Evil Practice." He reads about how Reiki invokes Japanese devils, and students of Reiki become unknowingly involved in this satanic practice of allowing evil forces to place a curse on the receiver of Reiki. One practitioner writes about how he soon realized that the initial energy he felt from Reiki eventually made him very sick. He suggests anyone who becomes involved in Reiki to go to church and pray for forgiveness.

Mason hasn't been to church in a very long time. He was brought up Christian and celebrates Easter and Christmas but does not attend church regularly. Now, he feels a strong urge to go to church, light a candle, sit in a pew before Christian icons, and pray to be cleansed for his multitude of sins. But is this really necessary? Mason tells himself that those articles are written by superstitious and religious extremists and decides his fatigue is due to his drained emotional state from earlier in the day.

He closes his eyes but soon hears a door open and is jolted up from his bed. Grabbing the bat, he keeps under his bed,

Mason slowly makes his way to the doorway of his bedroom and listens intently. Hearing nothing unusual, he nonetheless walks cautiously down the hall and looks into the family room.

Wait. There is rustling in the kitchen. Then Mason hears the sound of something metal hit the granite countertop. Someone is definitely in there. Mason imagines a burglar with a gun and stands frozen. He will have to sneak up on him and knock him out with his bat. He slowly takes another step forward to see a reflection on the oven door. He sees the reflection of a large man…but now there is laughing. Two people? The laughter is that of a man and a woman. Mason recognizes the laughter, but something isn't quite right.

Mason braces himself and then jumps out into the kitchen.

"What? What is this?" Mason asks in shock as he realizes who his uninvited guests are. He realizes the metal object he heard is a frying pan. Why is a carton of eggs out? Why is there a bag of groceries on the floor?

"Hi, Mason!" Skylar says.

"Skylar?" Her smile and seeing Skylar happy in his home lifts him so high he feels like he will burst with happiness. But his stunned adoration quickly fades as the realization of the man next to her comes into his focus.

Wesley moves close to Skylar, and then Skylar says, "We were just about to start making omelets with lots of herbs and roasted red peppers. Won't you join us?"

The sudden confusion makes Mason dizzy. This doesn't make sense. How can Skylar see Wesley? What are they doing together? Has Skylar forgiven him? What does all this mean?

"Wesley, what are you doing here?"

"We're in this together now, Mason."

"In what together? What are you talking about?"

Wesley smiles at Mason as he moves his arm around Skylar. Mason watches in horror as Wesley slides his hand down to Skylar's thigh and then begins to slide it up under her skirt.

Mason prepares to attack Wesley for touching Skylar so inappropriately but freezes when he sees Skylar throw her head back in an inviting gesture and smile as Wesley grabs her by the hair and plants his kiss on her neck. He lifts her up until she is sitting on the counter of the kitchen island with Wesley standing between her legs.

Why is he being punished this way?

"No. Stop it. Just stop it. Skylar? Skylar!" Mason begins to tremble as tears stream down his face, but he can't move. He just stands there, frozen and forced to watch as Wesley enters Skylar, and she lets out a moan.

Sweat. He is drenched in it. Mason's eyes pop open, and he sits up. The sheets are soaked. It was a dream. Mason feels relieved as he peels off his wet shirt and gets up to take a shower.

He realizes that he must have the flu. He feels weak and a little dizzy. Nonetheless, he showers and puts on a robe. The shower helps Mason feel awake. Hot tea will help. He makes his way to the kitchen and tries to shake off the images of Skylar and Wesley from his dream.

But he smells cigar smoke. Mason starts to sweat again as he looks around for Wesley. No sign of him anywhere. It must just be his imagination acting up after the dream…and he must be running a fever as well. Or is it Reiki that brings on that disturbing dream?

CHAPTER 18

OBSTACLE

Life is a daily battle with people and things that are trying to change us and those that are trying to prevent us from changing.

—Mokokoma Mokhonoana

Clean white shirt under a dark velvet sports coat, gray slacks, and leather boots. He throws on his winter coat. Mason picks up his keys for his Bugatti and decides a drive will help him clear his head. Not just a drive though, he needs a destination. He will go to church to light a candle and pray, something he hasn't done since he was a child.

The snow is coming down, and New York is covered in white. It's a little hard to see even with the windshield wipers on, but it feels good to be in this luxurious vehicle with its soft leather while the outside world is freezing cold. At a red light, Mason checks his reflection in the rearview mirror and is pleased that his eyes look clear and his hair is perfect. His smile fades as a puff of cigar smoke appears behind his reflection. Mason quickly looks back, and there he is: Wesley sits smirking and puffing a cigar.

A honking horn forces Mason to look forward again and push the gas pedal. "Stop messing with me, Wesley. I don't want you here."

"Now, now, my boy."

"I'm not your boy, Wesley."

"Where are you headed in this terrible weather? This weather is not fit for refined folks. Cold New York only makes me miss Charleston more. So tell me, where *are* you goin', Mason?"

"That's none of your business, Wesley. I told you I don't want you here, now get out!"

"Easy, my man. No need to take such a harsh tone. We may have had our differences but look at all the success I brought you. Without me, you have to agree that you're not so good at making movies. I said I'd make you famous, and I did. I kept my end of the bargain."

"*Your* end of the bargain? I don't remember bargaining with you, Wesley. You're not really here, not if I don't want you to be. My mind is my own. My soul is my own. Only I can decide which thoughts enter my mind and which ones I demand to leave. I am in complete control of my mind and soul. The only being that I will ever surrender myself to is God. God, help me."

Instantly, Wesley appears in the front passenger seat. He puffs his cigar, and the Bugatti fills with so much smoke it is hard for Mason to see where he is going.

Mason swerves as he struggles to see the road, and Wesley says, "Yes, your mind is your own and you allowed yourself to be led by me, that sealed the deal. Your soul is mine."

Mason takes his eyes off the road and looks at Wesley, who is grinning wickedly. He is about to say something when he completely loses control of the car to the icy road, snow, and cigar smoke. His body jerks forward, and he knows for only a millisecond that he crashes before all goes black.

CHAPTER 19

A CHANCE

We look forward to the time when the Power of Love will replace the Love of Power. Then will our world know the blessings of peace.
—William E. Gladstone

Mason feels the pain in his chest before he opens his eyes and hopes his injuries aren't as terrible as they feel. He wasn't wearing a seat belt and was propelled forward onto the steering wheel. Opening his eyes, Mason realizes that he is in a ditch off the side of the road. He touches the top of his head and doesn't feel any wetness or sticky blood, but then he looks in the rearview mirror and sees a scrape on his forehead. It's bleeding, but it doesn't look too terrible. He feels an ache in his mouth. Looking in the mirror, he smiles and sees his front tooth is broken. Shit.

Prying the door open takes a lot out of him as his chest aches terribly.

"I'm coming, hang on!" Mason hears a voice shout, and he looks up to see a woman running toward him.

The woman is wearing a white nurse's uniform, and when she's only a few feet away, Mason looks at her face and sees Skylar before realizing it is a young black woman he has never met before. Her uniform appears like something a nurse would wear in a WWI movie. Mason notices that she is carrying a black leather doctor's bag, also reminiscent of that era. Her hair, too, is styled in a puff, framing her heart-shaped face. Her eyes are steady, kind, and her expression unwavering. Looking at her, the term "wise beyond her years" comes to Mason's mind.

"You are going to be okay. I'm a nurse. My name is Octavia. What is your name?"

"Mason. Mason Hunter."

"Hi, Mason Hunter. Octavia Bridgewater. Put your arm around my neck, and I'll help you climb out of this ditch."

"No, I think I can drive it out of here."

"You are in no condition to drive. Plus, this car is not going anywhere in this slushy mess. Someone will come by and give us a lift soon enough. In the meantime, I'm just going to put something here to clean up this wound."

Octavia opens her doctor's bag, or nurse's bag, and pulls out a small, dark glass bottle with red liquid inside.

"Is that iodine?" Mason asks.

"Of course, it is. We don't want that open wound getting infected. I'm just going to dab a little bit here and hold on, let me get a bandage to cover it up. There."

"Thank you. I didn't know people still use iodine."

"Of course, we do. What else is there?"

"Other stuff. Whatever. Look, I'm going to try to get us out of here. I don't see anyone coming down the road, and it will be at least thirty minutes before a tow truck arrives. Aren't you cold out here without a coat?"

"Nah. I was born and raised in Helena, Montana. We've had our share of cold winters. It strengthens the blood."

"Is that so? Well, Octavia, if you don't mind coming around to the passenger side, I am going to drive us out of here."

Octavia pauses and studies Mason for a few seconds before walking to the front and around to the passenger side of the car.

Seated side by side, Mason maneuvers the Bugatti in drive and then in reverse, turning the steering wheel slowly as his chest aches.

"Let me help with the wheel. Tell me which way to turn it."

With Mason at the pedals and Octavia steering, the Bugatti nonetheless continues in an understeer skid.

"It's useless," Mason says in defeat. "So what do people in Helena do when they are stuck in a ditch?"

"We try to stay out of ditches," Octavia playfully replies. "Have you ever been to Montana?"

"Actually, no."

"It's the most beautiful state in the country. The majestic Rocky Mountains, clear Lake Helena, and the wild mountain flower-covered valleys. There is nothing like it anywhere else in the world."

As she speaks, Mason begins to feel an overwhelming sense of calm and peace. He looks over at Octavia, who begins to glow in a white light.

"Everything is going to be okay, Mason. I've been sent here to guide you."

"What? What do you mean? Sent by whom?"

"You asked for help, Mason."

Mason remembers praying right before the crash, but this seems too surreal. Octavia is glowing like an angel. He must be dreaming.

Suddenly, they are no longer sitting in the Bugatti. They are seated on the front porch of a house Mason does not recognize.

"Here we are. 502 Peosta Avenue. I'm going to tell you my story because it needs to be told. My story deserves to be heard, and now is the time for it to be shared with the world."

"Wait, I don't know what you think you can accomplish through me, but I'm in no position to trust another visitor who takes me on a strange journey into their past."

Octavia stands and gives Mason an understanding look with those caring eyes of hers and says, "It is always your choice to follow whoever you want to." She walks into the house, and Mason slowly takes his first step and proceeds to follow her.

Inside, a man, a woman, three boys, and two girls are sitting around a table in the home's kitchen.

"That's me," Octavia says as she points to one of the girls.

Mason sees the little girl in plain brown dress peeling potatoes. She sneaks a piece of bread from a plate next to her under the table to a small puppy.

"My father, Samuel Bridgewater, was the son of slaves. He was born in Tennessee and later enlisted as a Buffalo Soldier. He married my mom, Mamie Anderson, and they moved to Montana. After my father was wounded in the Spanish-American War, he retired, and my mom became a matron in the US Army Hospital. Papa died in 1912 when I was nine years old. Mama made sure that all of us kids helped take care of people, like she did. She was a leader in Helena's Second Baptist Church and the Helena Chapter of the Montana Federation of Colored Women's Clubs.

"I went to the Lincoln School of Nursing in New York City, which was one of only two nursing schools for African Americans. I received my registered nurse's degree from the University of the State of New York in 1930, but when I came back home to Helena, I discovered that a degree was not enough. Montana hospitals did not hire African American nurses.

"So, I kept up my work as a private-duty nurse, helping people any way I could. Then, in 1941, the Army Nurse Corps began accepting a small number of African American nurses, and I was one of only fifty-six black nurses accepted. As the need for nurses grew during an influenza epidemic, I fought for the rights of African American nurses, and more women of color were enlisted.

"As WWII began, the need for nurses continued to grow, and I served as the voice for all women nurses. Our work during the war gained us new respect as soon we were allowed full status as officers with full employment. After the war, St. Peter's Hospital in Helena began to hire black people, and I worked in the maternity department through the 1960s."

Mason follows Octavia as she walks back outside and around the back of the house. Mason gasps as the Rocky Mountains reveal their majestic glory in the distance. Octavia continues her story as the two stroll down a dirt path scattered with mountain flowers along the edges.

"One day in 1947, a woman in terrible labor pains was admitted to the maternity ward. Only seventeen years old and no more than five feet tall, she was terrified. I asked her if her mother was coming, and she replied that her mom died when she was a little girl.

"The doctor came in and examined her and then announced that the baby wasn't going to come for several hours. 'Plenty of time for me to go on a Sunday drive with my wife!' he said. The girl begged for him to stay, but he wouldn't listen to her. My heart went out to this girl.

"I rushed over to her after the doctor left and told her I would get her another doctor. And that's what I did. I called a doctor I knew who was resting at home from a skiing accident and explained to him that the baby is coming and that the other doctor left for a Sunday joyride. I stayed with her until the second doctor arrived. He put her out due to her pains. When she woke up, the young woman had a nine-pound baby!

"You see, Mason, most men, even doctors, didn't understand or empathize with women in labor. It was so important for nurses to be there and hold their hands, care for them, and be an extra set of eyes and ears when you have doctors like Dr. Sunday Joyride."

Mason listens carefully as he admires the beautiful landscape around him. They approach a running stream, and Octavia takes off her shoes and walks along the edge of the water. Being with her, Mason feels a kindred spirit. He feels at ease and free. He takes off his shoes and lets his toes sink into the warm earth beneath. Each step closer to the water fills him with happiness. A sun-filled breeze caresses his face, and he sees Octavia's chest glowing brighter.

"I understand, Octavia. I need to tell your story. Thank you for sharing it with me."

Suddenly, Mason is back in the Bugatti, alone. Lights in the rearview mirror reveal a tow truck has arrived to pull him out of the ditch.

CHAPTER 20

REDEMPTION

*God is the ultimate musician. His music trans-
forms your life. The notes of redemption rear-
range your heart and restore your life. His songs
of forgiveness, grace, reconciliation, truth, hope,
sovereignty, and love give you back your human-
ity and restore your identity.*

—Paul David Tripp

Mason works feverishly to complete the script for Octavia's
story. The purposeful fervor with which he works
reminds him of working alongside Skylar on *The Remake*. Did
God answer his prayers right before the crash? Did God send
Octavia to him with an idea for a movie that could help him
win back Skylar's love? After several hours of writing and rewrit-
ing, Mason closes his eyes and drifts into a sleep.

He is standing before the entrance of a cave. It's dark inside, and he looks behind him before heading inside. There is no one around. Mason proceeds to enter the cave, knowing that this is what he is there to do. As he walks blindly in the dark of the cave, he begins to hear the faint breathing of a sleeping being. The breathing is slow and steady, and as Mason continues walking, the breathing grows louder.

The breathing grows stronger and stronger, and then Mason feels the breathing inside his own chest. He lifts his head and looks down. His hands are claws. He raises his body and looks at his back to see two large wings. A few feet away stands Skylar, shouting something, but he can't hear. He attempts to call out her name but instead fire comes out.

He is a dragon. He kneels and waits for Skylar to climb his back. With Skylar on his back, Mason the dragon climbs out of the cave and begins to take flight but is yanked back. Skylar tumbles off, and he looks at his foot...it is chained to the cave.

Mason awakes to find Wesley sitting in a lounge chair next to the sofa where he had fallen asleep.

"What do you think you are going to accomplish with this little story of yours, Mason? Do you honestly believe anyone will want to watch a movie about a nurse who does what exactly? Becomes a nurse? Where is the drama? The suspense? There isn't any. This movie of yours will be another failure, just like your last one."

"Get out of here, Wesley. I told you, I'm done with you."

"But I'm not done with you, Mason."

"You don't belong here...now go!" And just like that, Wesley was gone...but his words remained.

Mason looks over at his computer where he had been working on the script for Octavia's story. He sits down before it and begins reading the script from the beginning. Would anyone really find this interesting? He had researched as much of Octavia's and the Bridgewater's lives as he could find. Then he elaborated facts with stories and characters of his own making to create a more personal and interesting perspective of the story. But now as he reads over his work, he really doubts the ability of his story to turn into a movie people could relate to. Another failure.

Sinking his head into his hands, Mason closes his eyes and tries to think of what to do next. How can he improve the script? Why is he undertaking this project? Because another ghost wants her story told? Isn't this how he got into this mess in the first place?

With his eyes closed, Mason sees a vision of Octavia in his mind...and the moment he first saw her, when he saw Skylar's face for a moment. Skylar, his one true love. Memories of Skylar come to him and how connected to each other they felt when they were working on the script for *The Remake* together. If only she is here now, she would know how to fix the script. Skylar knows exactly how to refine characters so that the audience can really connect with them.

Should he call her? No way. Skylar hates him and won't have anything to do with him, for sure. But what if this is his only chance? Skylar would love a story about an African American trailblazing woman early in US history. Yes! That's it! He has to call Skylar.

Taking out his phone, Mason's heart races as he goes to his contacts and finds Skylar's name. He hits send. The phone begins to ring.

"Hello?" Her voice is quiet.

"Skylar…hi, it's Mason. Please, don't hang up." Silence follows, and Mason feels hopeful since she is still on the line.

"I… I'm working on a script. It's something very special, and I think you would really like it, but I need your help getting it right."

"Mason. I'm sorry. But… I don't think that's a good idea."

"I know a lot has happened. But I've been getting help, and I'm better now. I just…this is the story you've been waiting for, Skylar. I can't do it without you…this is a story only you can tell in the way it's meant to be told."

After several seconds of silence, Mason realizes that Skylar is still listening, so he begins to relay the story of Octavia Bridgewater and her family. After he finishes telling Skylar as much about the script as he could, he waits, holding his breathe, as Skylar remains quiet.

Finally, she says, "I love it."

Hearing her say those words, Mason rejoices and smiles for the first time in weeks.

"But I can't work on it with you, Mason. I… I can't go back."

No, no, no. No, he can't lose her, or his life will be over. He has to keep going and won't stop until she agrees to work with him.

"Wait, Skylar. This isn't going back. I know I did terrible, unforgiveable things. I'm asking to work on this together, professionally. I could email the script to you, and you can share your thoughts, additions, and revisions, solely in email. You don't have to see me at all."

"I have to think about it, Mason," and she hangs up.

There's a chance she will accept. Mason quickly opens his inbox and composes an email to Skylar with the script for Octavia's story in an attachment. He hits send. That's all he can do for now. He leans back in his chair and takes a deep breath.

CHAPTER 21

JUDGMENT DAY

Love has within it a redemptive power. And there is a power there that eventually transforms individuals.

—Martin Luther King, Jr.

Skylar opens her MacBook and sees the email from Mason. What is she doing? Does she really want to be involved with Mason again? Professionally or not, she is treading on dangerous grounds. She doesn't trust herself around Mason. After everything they've been through, she still loves him. It doesn't make any sense. How could she love someone who hurt her the way he did? What if he tries it again? But she knows he is full of regret and will never let that happen again. Plus, he has been seeking professional help. Everything she knows about the mistreatment of women tells her that she must be suffering from battered woman syndrome. After all, isn't she just making excuses for her attacker? But this is different. Mason wasn't an abusive boyfriend. Rather, he had some sort of breakdown, and he is recovering from it.

But then she remembers Madison too. Could she forgive his unfaithfulness? And what he did to Zara? Could these also be explained away by a mental breakdown?

Skylar stares at the unopened email from Mason. She could just delete it. She could continue her life as it is, and one day she will meet someone new, and he will not be someone who has committed the crimes that Mason did. This new man in her life might be a doctor or a lawyer… Skylar tries to envision herself with a handsome stranger. She imagines a handsome man, someone who enjoys walks in Central Park, the Met, and the Frick House…he would also have to be mysterious enough to keep her interested, a little dangerous too…and then she knew she could never escape him. The only man she could see is Mason Hunter.

Clicking on the attachment, Skylar takes a deep breath and embraces her truth—that she is the one who can love the monster that is Mason Hunter. She begins to read the story of Octavia Bridgewater, which Mason titled *Heroine*.

ABOUT THE AUTHOR

Eleni P. Sianis was born in Chicago, Illinois. She attended Loyola University there and subsequently earned her juris doctorate from The John Marshall Law School. Sianis currently practices law in Illinois. She loves writing, books, and sharing that joy with her children. Particularly, Sianis enjoys books with complex characters, mysteries, and surprising twists. Sianis spent many summers in Greece growing up and continues to regularly travel and explore abroad with her husband and children.

CPSIA information can be obtained
at www.ICGtesting.com
Printed in the USA
LVHW010102220720
661195LV00006B/404